Middlemarch

GEORGE ELIOT

Level 5

Retold by Jane Rollason
Series Editors: Andy Hopkins and Jocelyn Potter

D1585944

52 909 72

Pearson Education Limited
Edinburgh Gate, Harlow,
Essex CM20 2JE, England
and Associated Companies throughout the world.

ISBN: 978-1-4082-9140-5

This edition first published by Pearson Education Ltd 2013

3 5 7 9 10 8 6 4 2

Text copyright © Pearson Education Ltd 2013
Illustration by Anna and Elena Balbusso

Set in 11/14pt Bembo
Printed in China
SWTC/02

Published by Pearson Education Limited in association with
Penguin Books Ltd, and both companies being subsidiaries of Pearson PLC

For a complete list of the titles available in the Penguin Readers series please go to
www.penguinreaders.com. Alternatively, write to your local Pearson Education office
or to: Penguin Readers Marketing Department, Pearson Education,
Edinburgh Gate, Harlow, Essex CM20 2JE, England.

Contents

Introduction

Until this meeting, Will had decided that Dorothea must be an unpleasant girl because she was going to marry Casaubon. But now he could only admire her beauty and her lovely voice and wonder why she was marrying his lifeless old cousin.

Middlemarch started life as two separate novels – one about a young woman called Dorothea Brooke and the other about a doctor called Tertius Lydgate. George Eliot was writing them at the same time and struggling with both, when she suddenly realised that they were two halves of the same story. The lives of Dorothea and Lydgate mirror each other, as they both search for a way to do good in the world. Eliot joined the two stories into one, moved it to a manufacturing town in the middle of England, and *Middlemarch* was born.

The novel follows Dorothea and Lydgate as they both go blindly into marriage, soon finding that the reality of married life is very different from their dreams. Even before her marriage, Dorothea is not interested in parties, expensive clothes or riding horses through the countryside. She prefers designing cottages for farm workers or finding good causes to spend her money on. She believes in the greatness of the human soul and thinks she has found it in the scholar, Mr Casaubon. She wishes to help him in his studies of the ancient world.

Lydgate is ambitious and full of new ideas, and wants to make discoveries in medical science. He wishes to understand and develop new treatments for fever, and even open a medical school in Middlemarch. He has chosen to work in a rural town to avoid the jealousies of London's medical world, but he soon finds that the country doctors are uninterested in new ideas. In love, he values beauty and a good singing voice more highly than sympathy and sense. He sees a wife as a decorative object, not a partner.

Dorothea and Lydgate both have faults and failings, but they deal with their disappointments in different ways.

George Eliot was born Mary Ann Evans on 22 November 1819, the youngest of three children, in rural England. Her father worked as an estate manager, like the character Caleb Garth in *Middlemarch*. Her mother was unaffectionate, but Mary Ann formed a close relationship with her brother, Isaac. After her mother died in 1836, she moved with her father to the manufacturing town of Coventry, where she cared for him until his death in 1849. Freed from family ties and changing her name to Marian, Eliot then travelled in Europe before settling in London. Unusually for women at the time, she worked as a journalist and translator, and became well known in London's free-thinking world of writers and artists.

In 1851 Eliot met and fell in love with George Henry Lewes (1817–78), a writer, philosopher and scientist. Their relationship was a true meeting of minds. Although Lewes was already separated from his wife, he was unable to make the separation legal and marry Eliot. Eliot and Lewes refused to give each other up, and began to live together as husband and wife. This was unusual at the time, and shocked her friends and family. Eliot's brother Isaac cut off all contact with her until after Lewes's death. London society was closed to her; Lewes received many social invitations, but they never included Eliot.

The happiness that Eliot had finally found with Lewes meant more to her than social success. They had no children of their own, but Lewes had sons from his marriage, and Eliot became a second mother to the boys.

As Eliot became more successful as a writer, people gradually accepted her unusual lifestyle. Sunday afternoon parties at her house, where the latest ideas of the day were discussed, became very popular. Eliot's novels were admired by almost everyone, including Queen Victoria.

Soon after Lewes died in November 1878, Eliot finally became a married woman. She married a friend, Henry Cross, who was twenty years younger than her. George Eliot died on 22 December 1880.

As soon as George Eliot was living happily with Lewes, she felt free to begin writing fiction. Her first novel was *Scenes of Clerical Life* (1857). From the beginning, Eliot's writing was original and truthful, describing life in the towns and countryside as it really was, and showing people's raw feelings and emotions. *Adam Bede* (1859), *The Mill on the Floss* (1860) and *Silas Marner* (1861) followed quickly and were all very successful. Her two late novels, *Middlemarch* and *Daniel Deronda* (1876) were longer, and more difficult for readers.

Middlemarch is the seventh of Eliot's eight novels. It was begun in 1869 and completed in 1872. It is one of the longest novels in the English language, and originally appeared in eight magazine parts over a year. The title means 'in the middle of our lives,' and is taken from the opening lines of Dante's *Inferno*. *Middlemarch* is about society, politics, agriculture, industry, the poor, wealthy landowners, religion, science and, most of all, human emotion and behaviour. It is a whole world.

There was already a nineteenth-century tradition of long novels painting a wide picture. Examples are *Vanity Fair* (1848) by William Thackeray, *Bleak House* (1852–3) by Charles Dickens (both available as Penguin Readers) and the *Barchester Chronicles* (1855–67) by Anthony Trollope. *Middlemarch* is different from these because its characters are more recognisable. Eliot helps us understand the thoughts and feelings of all the people in her novels; even the less important characters are shaped by events in the story. Everyone grows up, lives, fails or succeeds depending on their own efforts, chance and the actions of others whose paths they cross.

All eight novels appeared under the name of George Eliot. Marian Evans chose to write as George Eliot for two reasons. First, she wanted to protect her reputation as a journalist by using a different name for her novels. She could give up the name George Eliot if the public did not like the novels. Second, she chose a man's name because she did not want to be included among the many 'silly lady novelists' of her day. Women were not generally considered to be serious thinkers, as we see in *Middlemarch*.

The nineteenth century had, however, already produced some of the greatest women writers in the English language. Among the successful novels by women were *Pride and Prejudice* by Jane Austen, *Jane Eyre* by Charlotte Brontë, and *Frankenstein* by Mary Shelley (all available as Penguin Readers). Eliot's novels are different from these earlier books, however: her work explores history and politics, which Jane Austen's does not; she avoids the extreme creations of Charlotte Brontë, like mad Mrs Rochester locked upstairs; and she writes about what she knows, avoiding the science fiction world of Mary Shelley's Dr Frankenstein.

The events in *Middlemarch* take place between 1829 and 1832, a time of change in agriculture and industry, and in politics and society. In 1815, a new law had taken common land – open fields where the poor could farm – and given it to wealthy landowners like Sir James Chettam. After that, tenant farmers often had to depend on the good intentions of the landowner. Machines were coming into farming too, taking jobs that had been done by hand. Country people were forced to move into the towns, where they worked in new manufacturing industries, like the one owned by Mr Vincy in *Middlemarch*.

The arrival of the railways made this process faster. The working poor in the cities often lived in terrible conditions; the reforms that Mr Brooke supports were designed to help this situation. The French, just across the sea, had killed their king and formed a new kind of government, and Britain wanted to avoid the same kind of violent change. Political power was moving from the landowners who inherited their estates, like Sir Godwin Lydgate, to the middle classes, like banker Mr Bulstrode.

Eliot's partner Lewes was a scientist, and science, at the time, was progressing fast. Medical science is an important topic in *Middlemarch*; Lydgate argues for new ideas against the backward practice of country doctors. A new medical school had opened at University College London in 1828, and others were opening at London hospitals in the 1830s.

Women's lives were very different in the nineteenth century. Middle- and upper-class women had very limited lives. They could read and sew, walk in the woods and design gardens, but few went out into the world to work, and many people thought their ideas were of no value. Dorothea feels this most deeply, experiencing her life at Lowick Manor almost like life in a prison. She wants to help, but there is nothing for her to do. Eliot gives Dorothea more intelligence and higher morals than the other characters in the book, and shows how much talent society is wasting.

Above all, *Middlemarch* is a novel about how people behave, how they fall in and out of love, and how they want to make their mark in the world. If we travelled back to 1830s England, we would hardly recognise the lifestyle, but the thoughts and feelings of the people living then would be exactly like our own. For that reason, many people believe that *Middlemarch* is the greatest novel in the English language.

Chapter 1   Dorothea Brooke

The first thing that people noticed about Dorothea Brooke was her natural beauty. She always dressed plainly and wore her hair simply, and everybody said she was remarkably clever, although they usually added that her younger sister Celia was the more sensible of the two girls. They came from a good family, but were orphans and they lived with their unmarried uncle, Mr Albert Brooke, on a quiet country estate near the growing town of Middlemarch.

Dorothea, still only nineteen, was an idealist and wanted to do great things. She was more generous than her uncle, and she was impatient to reach the age of twenty-one, when she could spend her own money on improving the lives of others. She was wealthy; the sisters had both inherited money from their parents, and if Dorothea married and had a son, he would inherit Mr Brooke's estate. A man might hesitate to marry Dorothea, however, because occasionally her behaviour was unusual for a young lady. On one occasion, she knelt on a cold stone floor beside the bed of a poor sick worker and prayed for him. At other times, she refused food for twenty-four hours for the good of her soul, or sat up all night reading religious books. If she married, she might wake her husband one morning with a new plan to spend money on the poor – money that he might prefer to spend on horses.

Dorothea was beautiful, though, especially when she was on horseback. She loved the fresh air, and her eyes shone with the pleasure of riding. Everyone could see her beauty except her; she imagined that Celia was much prettier and that gentlemen visitors to Tipton Grange must be in love with Celia. Sir James Chettam, for example, was a regular caller. He owned the neighbouring estate, Freshitt Hall, a fine house surrounded by

1

excellent farmland, which he managed with the most recent ideas. Unlike Mr Brooke, he never minded spending money to improve his tenants' cottages or their farming methods. Dorothea considered Sir James the perfect husband for her sister. For herself, Dorothea imagined a husband with a great mind, who could teach her ancient languages and unlock the secrets of the past. It was unthinkable that *she* might marry a country gentleman like Sir James, who loved to hunt and fish, and agreed with everything she said without having any opinions of his own.

Sir James had been invited to dinner that day with a gentleman whom the girls had never met. According to their uncle, his name was Edward Casaubon, and he was a clergyman in the village of Lowick. He was also a scholar, and was writing an important work of religious history. He lived farther away than Sir James, so Mr Brooke had invited him to spend the night at the Grange.

As Mr Casaubon and Sir James took their seats at dinner, the contrast between the scholar and the country gentleman was extreme. Mr Casaubon had dark sunken eyes and was thin, pale and quiet. Little remained of his iron-grey hair. Sir James had thick red hair and a fresh face, and was always smiling.

'I am introducing some new farming practices among my tenants,' Sir James was saying. 'We are trying a new planting machine.'

'A great mistake,' replied Mr Brooke, thinking of the cost. 'You will make yourself into a poor man, Sir James.'

'It is not wrong to make yourself poor while trying to help others, Uncle,' said Dorothea. She spoke with more feeling than young women usually did, and Mr Casaubon looked at her with interest.

Mr Brooke turned to Mr Casaubon. 'Young ladies don't

understand economics,' he laughed. 'Nor history,' he continued, jumping immediately to a new subject. 'I am reading about Napoleon's wars. Does that subject interest you?'

'I have no time for recent history,' said Mr Casaubon. 'I spend my time reading ancient languages and wandering the ancient world like a ghost, trying to re-create it. And I have to take great care of my eyesight.'

Mr Casaubon spoke like a man making a public speech, but Dorothea was impressed. She thought that Mr Casaubon was the most interesting man she had ever met.

'You are such a fine horsewoman, Miss Brooke,' said Sir James to Dorothea, bringing the conversation back from the ancient world. 'I am sure you would enjoy hunting. I have just the horse for you – a lovely grey one. I was sorry to see you riding a very dull creature on Saturday. May I send the grey to you?'

Dorothea was annoyed. Why didn't Sir James talk to Celia instead of her, and let her listen to Mr Casaubon?

'Thank you, Sir James,' she said quickly. 'But I am going to give up riding.'

'Does your sister mean what she says?' Sir James asked Celia, looking hurt.

'Dorothea likes giving things up,' Celia said.

'I don't give things up to please myself, Celia,' said Dorothea. 'That would not be a good reason!'

'Do you believe that horse-riding is wrong?' said Sir James.

'I think it is wrong for me,' said Dorothea.

'Oh, why?' asked Sir James.

Mr Casaubon answered for her. 'We must not force Miss Brooke to give us her reasons,' he said. 'She knows that reasons can sound weak when they are put into words.'

Dorothea looked gratefully at Mr Casaubon.

'Of course,' said Sir James. 'I am sure that Miss Brooke's reasons are admirable.' He had noticed Dorothea's look of pleasure when Mr Casaubon rescued her, but the idea did not enter his head that this young girl would care for a dull scholar of nearly fifty.

Later, the two girls sat alone in their little sitting room.

'Mr Casaubon is so ugly!' said Celia.

'Celia!' said Dorothea. 'Why do you judge people by their appearance? Didn't you look into his eyes and see his great soul?'

'Has Mr Casaubon got a great soul?' asked Celia.

'Yes, I believe he has.'

The next morning Mr Casaubon told Dorothea more about his life's work, proving that all the world's myths came from the original Christian story. He had filled many notebooks, and his job now was to sort these notes into a book. He spoke to Dorothea as to another student, and he captured her heart. He seemed to her to be a wise and great man.

'We share the same ideas,' said Dorothea to herself. 'But his feelings and his experience are a lake compared with my little pool!'

After Mr Casaubon had driven off to his home at Lowick, five miles away from Tipton, Dorothea went out into the woods with her uncle's dog, Monk. She walked fast, and her eyes and cheeks shone. Like many single young women, Dorothea was thinking about marriage. Unlike many single young women, she was not thinking about wedding clothes or new furniture.

'I would study so I could help him in his work,' she said to herself. 'I would learn to see the truth and to think like great men. I would build modern cottages for the people of Lowick!'

At the exact moment when she was imagining life with Mr Casaubon, Sir James appeared on horseback with his servant and two hunting dogs behind him. He jumped to the ground.

'Miss Brooke!' he called. 'I was on my way to see you.'

Dorothea was annoyed at the interruption. And why wasn't Sir James on his way to see Celia? Dorothea simply did not realise that he was interested in *her* as a wife.

'I have brought you something which I hope you will admire,' said Sir James, holding out a tiny white dog.

'I don't like pets,' said Dorothea, making her opinion up as she spoke. 'Animals have souls like us. Either they should live freely in the wild, or they should be working animals, like Monk here. But I am sure that *Celia* likes these small pets.'

'You always have a clever opinion, Miss Brooke,' said Sir James, giving the unwanted dog to his servant. 'I would like to see your plan for workers' cottages on your uncle's land. I wish to build new cottages on my own estate. Your uncle thinks that such ideas are a waste of money, of course. The rent that the tenants pay will never cover the cost of building. But it is still worth doing.'

'Oh yes,' said Dorothea, looking at Sir James more affectionately. 'We live in beautiful houses while we let our tenants live in huts that are not good enough for pigs.'

At Tipton Grange, Dorothea showed Sir James all her plans. He took one away to show his estate manager, feeling that Miss Brooke's opinion of him had definitely improved.

A few days later, Mr Casaubon paid a morning visit and was invited again for dinner and an overnight stay the following week. Dorothea found that her first impressions were correct. She felt that his mind was her door to the mysteries of the past, and she loved the fact that he spoke only when he had something important to say. Her only disappointment was that he did not care about building cottages; whenever she started to talk about them, he changed the subject to the very narrow houses of the ancient Egyptians.

Sir James continued to visit much more often, and Dorothea was able to discuss her plans with him for as long as she wished. The building work soon started on his estate.

'Sir James is doing everything you wish,' Celia said to her, as they were driving home from Middlemarch one day. 'He wants to please you.'

'Not at all,' said Dorothea. 'He thinks of me as a future sister. I am sure he will ask you to marry him soon, Celia. Do you think you would accept him?'

Dorothea looked carefully at her sister to see the effect of her words. This was the first time that she had suggested Sir James as a possible husband for Celia, but she was sure that her sister liked him.

'You are making a mistake,' said Celia with some embarrassment. 'Sir James wishes to marry *you*. Everyone except you can see that he is in love with you.'

'No, that can't be right,' said Dorothea, but in a flash, she saw the truth. Was he only pretending to be interested in the cottages as a way of winning her good opinion? 'How could he think that I would accept him?' she cried. 'I have never agreed with him about anything except the cottages.'

'Well, I am sorry for Sir James,' said Celia with unusual courage and feeling. 'You never see what is quite obvious to everyone else.'

When they got home, Dorothea went straight to the library. She sat down to read, to take her mind away from Sir James and the cottages.

Mr Brooke soon followed her in and sat in a comfortable chair.

'Come and sit by the fire,' he said. 'I have something to tell you. I had lunch with Casaubon. I have known him for ten years now, since he came to Lowick. He buries himself in his books, and he has a lonely life. But he has a very high opinion of you, my dear. He knows you are only nineteen, and I said there was not much chance, but he wishes to make you an offer of marriage.'

'Thank you, Uncle,' said Dorothea after a long silence. 'I am very grateful to Mr Casaubon. If he asks me to marry him, I shall accept. I admire him more than any man I have ever known.'

Are you sure? He is a good choice in some ways. But Sir James would perhaps be a *better* husband? Have you thought of Sir James? And our land lies next to his. *You* must decide, but I believe that Sir James will also ask you to marry him.'

'It is impossible for me to marry Sir James,' said Dorothea. 'If he is thinking of asking me, he has made a great mistake.'

Mr Brooke realised that he had a lot to learn about women, even at his age. A fine man like Sir James had no chance at all!

'Well, Casaubon then. There is no hurry – for you. He, of course, is twenty-five years older than you. But if you like learning and that sort of thing ... And his income is good. He has inherited Lowick Manor from his older brother and his position in the Church is well paid. But he is not young, my dear, and his health is poor.'

'I don't want a husband near my own age,' said Dorothea decisively. 'I want a husband who has better judgement than me.'

'Ah? I thought you liked your own opinions.'

'I like to have opinions,' Dorothea agreed, 'but I also wish to have good reasons for them. A wise man would help me see which of my opinions were correct, and help me live according to them.'

Mr Brooke wanted to do the best for his niece, and was worried about her. 'Very true, but marriage can be a prison, you know. That is why I never married. And a husband likes to be master.'

'I never thought of married life as an easy life,' said Dorothea. 'I know that I must expect problems.'

'Well, you do not have the same tastes as other young ladies, my dear. You may prefer a religious man and a scholar. Sir James is a good man, you know, with a good heart, but he isn't known for ideas. But consider Casaubon's eyes. I think he

7

reads too much.'

'Then I can help him, Uncle,' said Dorothea, full of feeling.

'I see that you have made up your mind.' Mr Brooke handed a letter to his niece. 'This is for you. But there is no hurry, my dear.'

Dorothea shook with emotion as she read Mr Casaubon's letter. He wrote of his need for someone to help with his work and to make his hours away from his studies more cheerful. He said he had never expected to find such cleverness and religious feeling in a woman who was not yet twenty. If she agreed to marry him, he could offer her faithful love and a past without dark secrets.

As a love letter, it was not the best. But Dorothea did not think of questioning it; she thought only of a wonderful future, and she felt proud that a man like Mr Casaubon had chosen her.

The next morning, Dorothea sat with a book while Celia was sewing. Dorothea was not reading, however. She was staring out of the window and wondering how to tell Celia about her decision. She was afraid of Celia's reaction – perhaps because there was a tiny doubt in her own heart, a doubt that she felt but refused to listen to.

'Uncle tells me that Mr Casaubon is coming to dine today,' said Celia. 'I hope someone else is coming too. I don't wish to hear him eating his soup – he makes such a noise.'

'Celia, please don't make any more remarks of that kind,' said Dorothea. 'In fact, I have something to tell you. Mr Casaubon has asked me to marry him and I have accepted.'

Celia turned very pale. Tears came to her eyes. 'Oh, Dorothea, I hope you will be happy,' she said. 'I am sorry if I said anything to hurt you.'

'Please don't be sorry, Celia,' said Dorothea, trying not to feel hurt. 'You and I will never admire the same people.'

During Mr Casaubon's visit, Dorothea forgot her doubts.

She told her future husband how happy she was to be sharing in his life's work. Mr Casaubon was not surprised that he was the object of her feelings, and he did not ask himself if he was good enough for this beautiful girl. Dorothea did not ask herself if Mr Casaubon was good enough for her either; only if she could ever be good enough for him. The date of the marriage was fixed for six weeks' time.

On a grey November morning before the wedding, Dorothea made a visit to her future home, Lowick Manor, with her uncle and sister. Mr Casaubon lived in a large house with open gardens on one side, lined by fine old trees. Lowick Church could be seen from some parts of the garden, and green fields beyond that. The other side of the house was less attractive, even on a bright morning. The house was built in grey-green stone, with small windows, and looked sad. It needed children, bright flowers and open windows; instead, it was shaded by large groups of tall, dark trees, and Mr Casaubon's appearance at the door did not make the view more cheerful.

'Oh dear,' said Celia to herself. She thought of their visits to Sir James at Freshitt Hall, with its pretty white stone and beautiful flowers, and Sir James standing at the door, smiling like a prince. But Dorothea was very pleased with the dark bookshelves in the library, the old maps on the walls and the dull colours of the carpets and curtains.

Mr Casaubon led them to a little sitting room on the first floor, which looked out over the gardens and had pale blue furniture.

'This could be very pretty,' said Mr Brooke, 'with some new pictures and a little sofa, and a few things that young ladies like.'

'Please do not speak of changing anything, Uncle,' said Dorothea. 'There is so much in the world that *really* needs changing. And I am sure Mr Casaubon likes the room as it is.' She examined a group of small paintings on the wall. 'This must be your mother, Mr Casaubon,' she said, pointing to one of the pictures. 'But who is this, next to her?'

'Her elder sister, my aunt Julia,' answered Mr Casaubon. 'She made an unfortunate marriage and I never met her.'

Later, Mr Casaubon took his guests on a tour of the gardens and out into the village. There, they admired the church and the Lowick cottages, which were all in good condition. Each cottage had a vegetable garden, hens and a pig, and well-dressed children. Dorothea was disappointed, wishing that Lowick had a larger share of the world's unhappiness so she could do more good.

The group returned to the garden and took a path towards a fine old tree that stood alone on this side of the house. As they approached, they saw a young man, seated, drawing the tree.

'That is a cousin of mine,' said Mr Casaubon. 'He is the grandson of my Aunt Julia, whose picture we have just looked at upstairs.'

The young man laid down his drawing and came to meet them. He had light brown curly hair and grey eyes, like his grandmother.

'Dorothea,' said Mr Casaubon, 'let me introduce you to my cousin, Mr Ladislaw. Will, this is Miss Brooke.'

Will Ladislaw did not feel it necessary to smile at his cousin's future wife and her relatives; in fact, he had a look of discontent.

'You are an artist, I see,' said Mr Brooke, examining his drawing.

'Oh, this is not worth looking at,' said Will, his face turning red.

'This is nice. I did a little drawing myself at one time,' said Mr Brooke. 'What do you think, Dorothea?'

'I am no judge of these things,' said Dorothea, not coldly but not feeling able to give an opinion. 'Pictures are a language that I don't understand, Uncle.'

'You had a bad teacher, my dear,' said Mr Brooke. 'Girls should know about fine art – but you prefer drawing plans, of course.' He turned to Will. 'I hope you will visit my house, Mr Ladislaw, and I will show you my drawings.'

The young man did not answer Mr Brooke for a moment. Until this meeting, Will had decided that Dorothea must be an unpleasant girl because she was going to marry Casaubon. But now he could only admire her beauty and her lovely voice and wonder why she was marrying his lifeless old cousin.

'Mr Ladislaw,' repeated Mr Brooke. 'I hope you will visit me.'

'I am sorry, Mr Brooke,' said Will. 'Thank you for the invitation. Yes, of course, I would be delighted to visit you.'

Mr Casaubon and his guests returned to the house.

'What career is your cousin going to follow?' asked Mr Brooke.

'That is a painful subject,' replied Mr Casaubon. 'He refused to go to university in England, and studied instead in Heidelberg in Germany. Now he wishes to go abroad again, without any particular purpose, except what he calls culture.'

'He depends on you for money, I imagine,' said Mr Brooke.

'I have always paid for his education and have promised to get him started in a career,' said Mr Casaubon.

Dorothea looked at him with admiration. He was not asking for praise for his actions, simply doing what he thought was right.

'Will dislikes hard work and lacks the patience to learn law or medicine. I have pointed to my own notebooks, which represent years of hard work, and are just the preparation for a book I have not yet written. He says he does not wish to be tied to anything, like a horse working in the fields.'

'Will you allow him to go abroad again?' asked Mr Brooke.

'I have agreed to support him for a year or two,' said Mr Casaubon. 'He is leaving for Europe in a few days' time.'

Chapter 2   Dream and Reality

The people of Middlemarch and its surrounding villages had mixed opinions about medicine, and the arrival of a new young doctor gave them an excellent opportunity to express their views. Tertius Lydgate had bought the medical practice of old Dr Peacock, and came with a reputation for being wonderfully clever and particularly successful in his treatments of fever. He was the third son of a gentleman, which meant that he had good family connections but very little money. The oldest brother usually inherited the family estate, and younger sons went into professions. Lydgate had chosen medicine. He was among the guests at a party given by Mr Brooke, to celebrate the engagement of his niece Dorothea to Mr Casaubon.

When Lydgate was introduced to Dorothea, they found that they had similar interests and they discussed their ideas about improving workers' cottages and public hospitals enthusiastically.

'Mr Brooke,' called Lady Chettam, mother of Sir James. 'Please bring Mr Lydgate and introduce him to me. I wish to test him.'

Lydgate had developed the ability to look perfectly serious when nonsense was spoken to him. He agreed with Lady Chettam that her own medical history was unusual, saying that all medical histories were unusual but that hers might be more unusual than others. He listened to her views about strengthening medicines and dry hot-air baths, and said 'I think so' several times, and won Lady Chettam's good opinion. He left the party soon after that.

'Lydgate has lots of new ideas about fresh air and healthy eating,' said Mr Brooke, joining a group of Middlemarch gentlemen.

'I don't like new ideas,' said Mr Standish, an old lawyer. 'I like treatment that has already been tested.'

'Science and medicine need new ideas,' said Mr Bulstrode, a banker with an unhealthy appearance. 'I welcome Mr Lydgate, and I hope to put him in charge of the new hospital.'

'Good idea, Bulstrode,' said Mr Standish, who did not like the banker. 'Let him try his new treatments on your hospital patients. If a few of them die, I have no objection.'

'I believe in any treatment that cures me,' laughed Mr Vincy, a friendly factory-owner with a large waist, whose daughter was the prettiest girl in Middlemarch.

On the way home, Lydgate thought about Dorothea. Although her youthful beauty and her interest in cottages and the hospital had made a strong impression on him, she was not his idea of a perfect wife.

'She is a fine girl,' he thought, 'but too serious.' When Lydgate imagined himself at home with a wife, he was swimming in the pools of her blue eyes and listening to her heavenly piano playing, not discussing architectural plans or how to finance public hospitals. In fact, Lydgate had already noticed the most attractive girl in Middlemarch, who was very different from Dorothea. Her name was Rosamond Vincy, daughter of Mr Vincy.

He had first met Rosamond by chance when he was attending one of his patients. Mr Featherstone lived at Stone Court, near Lowick, and Rosamond and her brother Fred were sitting with the old man, their uncle, who had not long to live. Mr and Mrs Vincy hoped that Mr Featherstone would leave his house and most of his fortune to young Fred, and they encouraged both Fred and Rosamond to visit Stone Court as often as possible. Everything about Rosamond delighted Lydgate; her tiny waist, her perfect manners, and the way she moved her beautiful head.

'Rosamond has been singing to me,' said old Mr Featherstone, lying in his bed. 'I hope you have nothing against that, Doctor.'

'Look at the time,' said Rosamond, standing up and reaching for her hat. 'It is later than I thought. Fred, we must go.'

'Miss Vincy is a musician?' observed Lydgate with interest, following her with his eyes. Rosamond knew that she was being watched, and put her fingertips to her blonde curls.

She moved towards her hat, which lay on a table by the door. Lydgate was quicker, however, reaching the hat first and turning to present it to her. Their eyes met, and both felt that they were seeing clearly for the first time. This moment, Rosamond believed, was called 'falling in love'. She had imagined such a scene many times since she had first heard of the arrival in Middlemarch of a clever young doctor from a good family. It was not his good looks or intelligence that attracted her, but the fact that there was a baronet in his family. She did not like being the daughter of a manufacturer, and the granddaughter of a man who owned a pub, and she dreamed of marrying into a higher level of society.

Lydgate was as ambitious as Rosamond, but in a different way; he was anxious to make a reputation for himself in the medical world. At twenty-seven years of age, he hoped to achieve great things in his life, and, like Dorothea, he was an idealist. He had wanted to study medicine since, as a boy, he had opened a large, dusty book about the human body and been amazed by the pictures of the world inside his little body. He had studied in London and Paris, but now he planned to earn his living in a quiet country town, away from the childish jealousies and showy successes of London, and find a new way of treating fever. Lydgate dreamed of making a great discovery, and of adding to the store of human knowledge.

The medical profession was in great need of reform. Much medical practice consisted of giving many drugs to patients; the public believed that the more drugs they swallowed, the more likely they were to be cured. Doctors either sold the drugs directly to their patients, or sent them to the chemist, who paid the doctor an agreed sum. One of Lydgate's ideas was to take no money for any drugs he ordered, an idea that was unlikely to make him popular among the other doctors. But he had his faults. He felt superior to his country colleagues in his education, manners and dress.

Not long after Mr Brooke's party, when Dorothea had become Mrs Casaubon and was on her way to Rome with her new husband, Lydgate found himself in the office of Mr Bulstrode, the banker. Mr Bulstrode was a very religious man who did not seem to enjoy any of life's physical pleasures and who never hesitated to point out other people's mistakes. As a small-town banker, he knew the financial secrets of most of the manufacturers and tradesmen in the town, which made him very powerful and very unpopular.

He was especially disliked by those Middlemarchers who felt that eating a fine meal, drinking one or two glasses of wine or placing a small bet on a game of billiards were not the actions of the Devil.

The banker's moral views were of no interest to Lydgate, however, who simply observed to himself that Bulstrode did not look well. They were discussing the new hospital, which was nearly finished, and of which Mr Bulstrode was one of the main financial supporters.

'I am very pleased to put you in charge of the new hospital,

Mr Lydgate,' said the banker. 'My own poor health has led me to get advice from doctors here in Middlemarch and in London. Medical skills in Middlemarch are low, sir, very low. I hope you will have the courage to earn the dislike and jealousy of the medical profession in Middlemarch by bringing reform.'

'That is exactly what I plan to do,' smiled Lydgate. 'I am aware that most country doctors know little of scientific progress. I hope we can create a fine hospital, specialising in fevers, an area in which I have some knowledge. Perhaps one day we can open a medical school here.'

'I hope, Mr Lydgate,' said Mr Bulstrode, 'that you recognise the spiritual needs of your patients as well as their physical needs? The hospital must have a clergyman. The new hospital building is very near the church of Mr Farebrother. Do you know Mr Farebrother?'

'Yes, he seems a very intelligent, pleasant man. I understand he is interested in natural science – especially insects.'

'I don't like Mr Farebrother's way of preaching,' said Mr Bulstrode. 'I wish to appoint Mr Tyke as the new hospital's clergyman. There will be a vote, and not all the directors like Mr Tyke. My wife's brother, for example, Mr Vincy, prefers Mr Farebrother. You will have a vote, Mr Lydgate, and I hope you will support me.'

In fact, the subject of the vote was discussed again at Mr Vincy's table when Lydgate was dining there at Rosamond's request.

'Tyke is dull,' said Mr Vincy, 'and Farebrother is good company and an excellent preacher. Farebrother has my vote.'

After dinner, Lydgate and Rosamond sat together on the sofa. Rosamond's small feet, perfect shoulders and clever conversation had a magical effect on Lydgate.

'I am sorry that I didn't hear you sing at your uncle Featherstone's,' said Lydgate, admiring her blonde curls against

16

her sky blue dress. 'Will you let me hear some music tonight?'

'Papa always asks me to sing,' said Rosamond. 'But you have heard the best singers in London, and you will make me nervous.'

'Have you been to London?' asked Lydgate.

'Only once,' she said. 'I saw a few of the ordinary sights that simple country girls are always taken to.'

'Do you call yourself a simple country girl?' asked Lydgate, admiring her long neck.

'I mean I am not as well educated as you,' she said. 'I am not usually afraid of talking to anyone, but I am really afraid of you.'

At that moment, Mr Vincy opened the piano on the other side of the room and called his daughter. As she played and sang, her soul seemed to wrap around Lydgate's heart.

Later, Mr Farebrother arrived. He was a handsome man, aged about forty, and while his black clergyman's clothes were past their best, his quick grey eyes attracted attention. He had a special word for everyone in the room, and seemed to say more in ten minutes than had been said during the rest of the evening. Lydgate stood up to leave.

'You will find us very stupid in Middlemarch, I feel sure,' Rosamond said. 'You must be used to something quite different.'

'I suppose all country towns are similar,' said Lydgate. 'I have made up my mind to accept Middlemarch with all its faults, and I hope the town will accept me in the same spirit. I have certainly found some of its charms to be much greater than I expected.'

Rosamond turned away, her cheeks burning red with pleasure.

As he walked home, Lydgate thought about Rosamond and her music. He liked her very much, but he did not wish to marry for several years, so he did not imagine that he was in love with her. As soon as he reached home, he lost himself in a new book on fever, reading into the early hours of the morning and not giving a second thought to love and marriage.

Some weeks later, the directors of the old hospital met to vote on the appointment of the clergyman for the new one. Lydgate had spent an evening with Mr Farebrother, examining his collection of insects, and thought him a good-tempered, honest man, kind to his mother, aunt and sister, who all depended on him at home. Lydgate wished to be his friend and did not look forward to voting against him.

'Don't worry about my feelings,' Mr Farebrother said to Lydgate. 'If you vote against Tyke, Mr Bulstrode won't hesitate to end your involvement with the new hospital. He won't be friends with anyone who goes against him.'

So Lydgate examined his thinking. There were reasons against voting for Mr Farebrother: the man had no free time – and he played billiards in a Middlemarch pub for money, which Lydgate did not approve of. Mr Tyke, on the other hand, had time for the extra work. Nobody had anything to say against him, except that they did not like him and they suspected him of being a hypocrite. Lydgate was not happy. People would say he was voting with Mr Bulstrode for his own advantage. Of course he did not care about the banker's friendship, but he did care about getting a good hospital. For the first time Lydgate was experiencing small town politics, and he found them annoying.

Before the meeting started, the men of Middlemarch expressed their opinions noisily. Some supported Mr Farebrother and others supported Mr Tyke; none liked Mr Bulstrode, and all agreed that Lydgate would do what the banker told him. When Mr Bulstrode and Mr Brooke arrived, everyone sat down. A short, bad-tempered discussion followed before each person wrote 'Tyke' or 'Farebrother' on a piece of paper. While the votes were being counted, Lydgate arrived.

'The votes are equally divided,' said Mr Bulstrode after the count, looking at the young doctor. 'The final decision is yours, Mr Lydgate.'

This was the worst possible situation for Lydgate. If he had arrived on time, nobody would have seen his vote. Now all attention was on his hand, as his pencil hung above the piece of paper. He wrote down 'Tyke'.

♦

Dorothea and Mr Casaubon had now been in Rome for five weeks. Mr Casaubon had spent much of each day studying in the Vatican library, but they had also visited the most important museums, the best viewpoints, the greatest ruins, and the finest churches and palaces. Dorothea had seen little of the world until now, and the contrast between the riches of the past and the poverty on the streets was confusing. The reality of her married life was confusing too. What was different? Mr Casaubon acted and spoke in the same way as before, and he had never pretended to be something he was not. But in these five weeks, Dorothea had felt a terrible depression; the wide fields of knowledge and fresh ideas that she had dreamed of finding in her husband's mind were actually dark little rooms and long passages that led nowhere. His comments on everything they saw were dull and lifeless, and left her feeling ice cold.

Dorothea only wanted him to be affectionate towards her. She wanted him to ask her about her past life, or to tell her about his past. She wanted him to enjoy her warm kisses, but he showed no more feeling than a piece of wood.

'My work has taken longer than I expected,' said Mr Casaubon, as he finished reading his letters, one morning, 'but I hope you have not spent the time unhappily.' He smiled. He had not found marriage a heavenly existence either, but he knew his duty as a husband. He must make his charming young wife as happy as possible.

'Are you satisfied with the work you have done here?' asked Dorothea, trying to keep her mind on her husband's interests.

'Yes,' he said. 'It has been slow, but you have stopped me thinking too much about it outside my hours of study.'

'I am very glad that my presence has made a difference to you,' said Dorothea. She thought of those evenings when Mr Casaubon had seemed hardly conscious after his day of study. There was even a little anger in her voice. 'I hope that when we get to Lowick, I will be more useful to you, and be able to take part in your work.'

'No doubt, my dear,' said Mr Casaubon. 'The notes I have made here will need sorting.'

'And all your notes in the library at Lowick,' said Dorothea, her heart burning inside her and her voice rising. 'Will you decide which parts to use, and begin to write the book which will bring your knowledge to the world? I will find the notes you need and write them out: I can be of no other use!'

While Dorothea's show of emotion alarmed Mr Casaubon, her words cut him deeply. She was as unaware of his inner worries as he was of hers. She heard her own heart beating violently, but she did not hear his. To Mr Casaubon, this young wife suddenly appeared like a spy for his cruellest critics. Instead of watching with admiration as he covered page after page with his pen, she had blindly stuck a knife into that place in his soul where he hid the truth: the fact that he could never write his great work.

'My love,' he said, his face red with anger for the first time in their married lives. 'I cannot accept criticism of my work from someone who knows nothing about it. If a subject lies beyond a mind's reach, the owner of that mind should remain silent.'

'Of course I know nothing about it,' said Dorothea. 'I am simply stating the fact that I have seen your notes, but I have not seen any chapters from the book. I only wish to help you.'

Mr Casaubon watched in shock as Dorothea left the room. He tried to read a letter that lay on the table, but he could not. He had never imagined married life to be like this. Neither had Dorothea.

Later that morning, in the Vatican museum, Dorothea stared at a picture of the Greek goddess Aphrodite, but she was not seeing Aphrodite. She was imagining the joyless years of her future life at Lowick. Suddenly, she became conscious of two strangers behind her. She turned away without looking at them, and left the room.

'She is the most perfect Madonna I have ever seen,' said a young German, unable to take his eyes off her. 'I must paint her Ladislaw. Let us follow her home.'

'No,' said Will Ladislaw. 'I know her. She has recently married my cousin. But I didn't know they were coming to Rome.'

'But that is even better – you know them, you can ask them if they will allow me to paint her.'

'No, Naumann!' said Will. 'I have only met her once, for a couple of minutes, before I left England. And how can you ever capture in paint a real woman, who changes from moment to moment. Mrs Casaubon, for example, the woman we have just seen – how would you paint her heavenly voice?'

'I see,' said the good-natured Naumann. 'You are jealous.'

'Nonsense,' said Will, but Naumann was right.

Two hours later, Dorothea was sitting in the apartment in the Via Sistina, crying bitterly. Safely alone at home after returning from her visit to the Vatican with her husband, where he remained in a spidery corner, she had allowed her unhappiness to burst out. A sudden knock at the door made her dry her eyes quickly.

'Mr Ladislaw is here,' said Dorothea's servant.

'Oh,' said Dorothea, 'please show him into the sitting room.'

She waited a minute or two, allowing the tears to dry on her face and feeling that this was a useful reminder of her husband's goodness. As she thought of Mr Casaubon's generosity to his cousin, her feelings of discontent with her marriage melted. She entered the room with a warm smile and held out her hand to Will.

'I wasn't aware that you and Mr Casaubon were in Rome,' said Will, feeling suddenly shy. 'I saw you at the Vatican this morning. I hope ... I mean ...'

'Please sit down,' said Dorothea, trying to help him relax. 'Mr Casaubon is very busy, but I am sure he will want to see you.'

'Here is my address,' said Will, holding a card out to Dorothea and noticing the signs of tears on her face. 'I will come again tomorrow when he is likely to be at home.'

'He goes to read in the Vatican library every day, and you are unlikely to see him unless you make an appointment. Especially now. We will soon leave Rome, and he has a lot to do. But I am sure he will invite you to dinner.'

Will could not speak for a few moments. First, his dull cousin had persuaded this lovely creature to marry him, and now he was spending his honeymoon away from her, preferring to follow dusty paths of useless study. Will struggled to control his desire to laugh or to shout in anger.

Dorothea noticed his amusement. 'You find something funny?' she asked.

'I am thinking of our last meeting,' he said quickly. 'You destroyed my poor drawing with your criticism.'

'Surely not,' said Dorothea. 'I know nothing about painting.'

'You thought it was a poor representation of the countryside,' said Will, smiling broadly.

'That was my lack of knowledge,' said Dorothea, enjoying Will's good humour. 'I have gone around Rome in the same way. I have seen so much, but I have not understood half of it.'

'I have begun to understand great art a little better since I started painting myself,' said Will.

'Will you be a painter?' asked Dorothea. 'As a career, I mean.'

'No,' said Will. 'I haven't got the talent or the patience to learn. If things don't come easily to me, I give them up.'

'Mr Casaubon believes you need more patience,' said Dorothea, rather shocked by Will's idea of treating life as a holiday.

'I know his opinion,' said Will. 'He and I are very different.'

'I wasn't comparing you,' said Dorothea, offended by something in Will's voice. 'There are few men who can spend their lives following one goal as Mr Casaubon does.'

'You are right,' said Will. 'It is a pity that his hard work is wasted, like so much English scholarship. If Mr Casaubon read German, he would save himself a lot of trouble.'

'What do you mean?' asked Dorothea, suddenly anxious.

'The Germans have taken the lead in historical enquiries and they have already done the work. They covered the ground that Mr Casaubon is studying twenty years ago. I have spoken to Mr Casaubon about it, but he doesn't listen.'

Will had no idea how much his words wounded poor Dorothea.

'Why didn't I learn German when I was at school in Switzerland?' she said. 'Now I can be of no use.'

Will suddenly understood that Dorothea had built up a romantic idea of life with a scholar. She must know already how wrong she had been. At that moment, Mr Casaubon himself entered the room. He was surprised to see Will, and not at all pleased, but greeted him politely. He could see immediately that his young cousin's sunny brightness delighted Dorothea, and he was jealous. His feelings did not show on his dull face, however, and Dorothea's cheerful mood was not affected. Will's visit had lifted her spirits. She had never met anyone as quick and bright as him, and so likely to understand everything she said.

After Will left, Dorothea apologised to her husband for their disagreement at breakfast. Mr Casaubon accepted her apology, did not apologise himself and nothing more was ever said about it between them. But Dorothea never forgot it.

Dinner the next evening was delightful, and even Mr Casaubon seemed to become more cheerful. Will made himself very pleasant to Mr Casaubon, bringing him into conversation and agreeing with many of his opinions. He offered to take Mr Casaubon and Dorothea to one or two artist's workshops before they left the city; it was, he said, a Roman experience that should not be missed.

The following day, Will led them to the door of his German friend, Adolf Naumann, whom they found hard at work on a religious painting. His pictures were arranged around the room. The painter presented his work to his visitors, before making a request.

'My friend Ladislaw says that you won't mind, sir, if I ask permission to copy your head,' said Naumann in his confident English, and he showed Mr Casaubon one of his paintings. 'I need a model for St Thomas Aquinas★ in this picture.

'I am amazed,' said Mr Casaubon, an unusual brightness suddenly appearing on his tired cheeks. 'If my poor head can help you with such a great man, I would be honoured – if Mrs Casaubon doesn't object to the delay.'

★ St Thomas Aquinas (1225–74): an Italian churchman and philosopher

'It is a wonderful idea,' said Dorothea, not noticing the little smile that Naumann directed at Will behind Mr Casaubon's back.

She sat down to watch, feeling happy for the first time on her trip to Rome.

Soon Naumann needed to allow the paint to dry for half an hour before continuing.

'Perhaps while we are waiting, sir, I could do a little painting of your wife,' he suggested.

'Where shall I stand?' said Dorothea at once, before Mr Casaubon could object.

'I want you to be St Clare*,' said Naumann.

As Will watched Naumann arranging Dorothea's arms, he wanted to fall at her feet – and to knock his friend down.

At the end of the visit, Mr Casaubon was so pleased with his Aquinas that he arranged to buy the picture and have it sent to Lowick.

The following day, Will called to see Dorothea when he knew that his cousin was at the library. Dorothea was not aware that Will's appearance in Rome had displeased her husband, and received him happily. She showed him some jewels that she had chosen for her sister Celia, who had just become engaged to Sir James Chettam.

'I wished to have you with us when we chose them this morning,' said Dorothea, smiling. 'But Mr Casaubon said that there wasn't time. He will finish his work tomorrow, and we are leaving in three days.'

Will agreed that they were fine choices, and took a seat opposite Dorothea. They discussed art, often disagreeing, but delighted with each other's conversation. Will believed that art, nature and poetry were the bread of life. To Dorothea

★ St Clare (1194–1253): a religious woman. She formed a group of women who gave up wordly pleasures, prayed, and worked with their hands.

art seemed unimportant next to the world's social problems, and she was upset by the fact that most people would never experience art.

'You are so full of ideas and life,' Will burst out. 'And now you will be shut up in that stone prison at Lowick; you will be buried alive. It makes me wild to think of it!'

He stopped speaking, feeling that he had said too much.

'Please don't worry about me,' said Dorothea, smiling. 'I have chosen Lowick for my home.'

They were both silent for a moment. Dorothea returned to the subject of Mr Casaubon's work. She wondered why her husband's ideas were not useful in the way that, for example, Leonardo da Vinci's ideas were still useful, hundreds of years after his death.

'The subject that Mr Casaubon has chosen changes as quickly as chemistry,' said Will lightly. 'The ideas he is studying are already out of date. What use is that to anybody?'

'Why are you smiling?' asked Dorothea. 'It hurts me to think that a good scholar like Mr Casaubon might fail in his life's work. Oh, I don't know what I am saying.' Dorothea was shocked by her own words, and angry with Will for leading her to them.

'I agree with you,' said Will. 'And that is why *I* won't fail. Mr Casaubon's generosity has given me a dangerous freedom, but I now intend to return to England and depend on nobody except myself.'

'That is excellent news,' said Dorothea, her good mood returning. 'Mr Casaubon will be very pleased.'

Will stood up, ready to leave.

'I am so glad we met in Rome,' said Dorothea.

'I made you angry,' said Will. 'You will think badly of me.'

'No, I like you very much,' said Dorothea. 'I am interested to see what you will do.

That evening, Dorothea told her husband about Will's plans, and asked him if he was pleased.

'I have a duty towards him,' said Mr Casaubon coldly. 'His future career is of no interest to me apart from that.'

Dorothea did not mention Will again.

Chapter 3   Another Wedding

'Mr Lydgate! Mr Lydgate!' called a voice. Lydgate was crossing the street outside the Vincys' house, and turned to see Mrs Vincy waving wildly at him from a downstairs window. Moments later, he was trying to calm the unhappy woman.

'My poor boy is ill!' said Mrs Vincy, tears pouring down her face. 'Dr Wrench has been and has sent some medicine, but now Fred is worse, and Dr Wrench can't be found.'

Rosamond, who had first spied Lydgate through the window, waited long enough for him to notice that she was prettily anxious for her brother, before leaving the room.

Lydgate examined Fred, who was sitting by the fire and shaking. He was sure that the young man was in the early stages of a serious fever and that Wrench had given him the wrong medicine. He gave Fred the correct medicine, sent him upstairs to bed immediately, ordered a nurse to be employed and gave strict instructions for no visitors. Mrs Vincy's terror – and her unhappiness with Wrench – increased with every word

'*You* must look after Fred,' cried Mrs Vincy. 'I cannot have my boy left to a doctor who may or may not come.'

'I will meet Dr Wrench here,' said Lydgate, aware that he was not making friends among the Middlemarch medical profession.

Mr Vincy arrived home then, and was very angry with Wrench. 'I will tell him what I think when I see him, whether he likes it or not.'

Wrench did not like it. Lydgate was polite to his colleague when they met at the Vincys, but that only made it worse for Wrench; he had no desire to be instructed by a younger man with foreign ideas. Wrench refused to visit the Vincys again, and Lydgate became their doctor, an event that was much discussed in Middlemarch.

The younger Vincy children and their nurse were sent away to escape infection, but Fred's illness and Wrench's mistake had brought Lydgate to Rosamond, and she had no intention of leaving.

Mrs Vincy had no interest in anything except her boy; when Fred cried out nonsense in his fever, it broke her heart. She followed Lydgate out of Fred's room whenever he visited, put her hand on his arm and said quietly, 'Save my boy!'

As Mr Vincy was often away from the house at work and Mrs Vincy was always with Fred, Rosamond found herself alone downstairs when Lydgate arrived or departed. Lydgate never stayed long with her, but an understanding developed between them during their moments together.

Fred gradually improved, and the atmosphere in the house became more cheerful. Friends and family were invited again, and Lydgate often stayed to listen to Rosamond sing.

Lydgate seemed almost perfect to Rosamond, and so different from the young men of Middlemarch. Some wore fine shoes and silver rings, but they could not speak a word of French, had no manners, and knew only about farm machinery. Lydgate was superior in every way. When he spoke, everyone listened. Whatever the occasion, he wore the right clothes. Rosamond was proud when he came to sit beside her, making other young men jealous.

Lydgate enjoyed her company more and more. Apart from Mr Farebrother, he found Middlemarch men dull; he had no interest in commercial politics or card games, so how could he relax?

They were playing at being in love, but with different rules. Lydgate had no intention of marrying, while Rosamond had already chosen a handsome house in the town for their married home.

♦

As Mr and Mrs Casaubon returned to Lowick Manor from their honeymoon in Rome in the middle of January, snow was falling. Dorothea looked out at the frozen ground from her sitting room window, and thought about her married life. Everything was done for her, nobody asked for her help, and although she was recently married, there were no sweet moments of love to fill her hours. The ideas and hopes that had lived in her mind three months before were now only memories. She looked around the little blue-green room, until at last she saw something with new meaning. It was the tiny picture of Mr Casaubon's Aunt Julia – Will's grandmother.

Over the next few weeks, Dorothea helped her husband every morning in the library, either copying out notes or reading aloud to preserve his eyesight. One morning, when she came in early, Mr Casaubon was not in a good mood.

'Dorothea, here is a letter for you,' he said. 'It was inside a letter addressed to me.'

'It is from Mr Ladislaw! What can he have to say to me?' she said, sounding pleased. 'What does he say to you?'

'He wishes to visit us,' said Mr Casaubon coldly. 'But I must tell you that I am too busy for such a visit, and I must refuse.'

There had been no angry words between them since Rome, but Dorothea felt that her husband was being unfair.

'At least wait for me to do something wrong,' said Dorothea. 'Have I said that I would like to see Mr Ladislaw against your wishes?'

'We will say no more on the subject,' said Mr Casaubon. 'I have neither time nor energy for this kind of conversation.' He tried to write, but his hand shook too violently.

Dorothea left Will's two letters unread on her husband's desk and went to her own place feeling superior. She began to copy out some Latin notes, her hand steady and her mind clear. She had not looked up from her desk for half an hour when she heard the loud bang of a book on the floor. She turned quickly and saw Mr Casaubon holding the back of his chair and in danger of falling. She ran to him and helped him to a chair as he struggled for breath.

By the time Lydgate arrived, Mr Casaubon was more comfortable. It was a heart attack, but it was not serious, and he began to recover at once. Lydgate visited every day for the next week, finding Dorothea sitting anxiously beside her husband each time. One day, as he was leaving, he asked to speak to her alone.

'Mr Casaubon has recovered more quickly than I expected,' said Lydgate. 'But we cannot always say how such cases will progress.'

'Please speak plainly,' said Dorothea. 'I must know everything.'

'He may live for fifteen years or more, without his health becoming worse.'

'You mean if we are careful,' said Dorothea, turning pale.

'Yes – there must be no worry, and he must not work so hard. We may be lucky, and there may be no further attack. On the other hand, death can be very sudden.'

'You are a wise man,' said Dorothea. 'You know all about life and death. What can I do?'

'What do you think of foreign travel?' asked Lydgate.

'Oh no,' said Dorothea. 'He doesn't enjoy travel.'

'Then I don't know what to suggest,' said Lydgate. 'Please don't say anything about our worries to Mr Casaubon. The anxiety would make his condition worse.'

'He has worked hard all his life,' said Dorothea, her eyes filling with tears. 'He cares about nothing else. *I* care about nothing else.'

Lydgate had never met a woman like Dorothea, and he never forgot this moment, when Dorothea's soul cried out to his. But there was nothing he could say.

Left alone in the library, Dorothea dried her tears. She looked around the room, thinking that she must ask the servant to tidy Mr Casaubon's desk. She saw Will's letters and decided to read them in case it was necessary to write and prevent the unwanted visit.

Will wrote from Rome. He thanked Mr Casaubon for generously paying for his education. He explained that he was coming to England to find a job, and would no longer need financial help from his cousin. He hoped to deliver Naumann's painting to Lowick in person. His letter to Dorothea continued their discussion in Rome about art, but she found it too painful to read.

Dorothea decided to ask her uncle to reply to Will and tell him that Mr Casaubon had been ill, and they could not receive any visitors at Lowick. Mr Brooke was always happy to write a letter; his only problem was in writing a short letter. By the time he had covered three pages, he had invited Will to visit him at Tipton Grange. As Celia would soon marry Sir James Chettam and leave Tipton, Mr Brooke felt that a young man who was interested in politics would be excellent company at his dinner table. He was sure Dorothea would not mind, and in fact he forgot to tell her.

♦

That same evening, Lydgate visited the Vincys and sat with Rosamond.

'Mrs Casaubon has very strong feelings for Mr Casaubon,' he said, 'although he must be at least thirty years older than her.'

'Of course she loves her husband,' said Rosamond, thinking it was not so bad to have Lowick Manor and a husband who was likely to die soon. 'Do you think she is very beautiful?'

'She is certainly beautiful, but I haven't thought about it.'

'You are too professional,' said Rosamond. 'And how successful you are in Middlemarch! First Lady Chettam and now the Casaubons are your patients.'

'Yes, I like Mrs Casaubon very much, but as a general rule I prefer to look after the poor,' said Lydgate. 'Their cases are more interesting, and one doesn't have to listen politely to nonsense.'

'At least you are in grand houses that don't smell,' she said.

'That is true, my fine lady,' smiled Lydgate.

Like a honey bee around a flower, Lydgate was always at Rosamond's side. Their relationship was the talk of the town, and only the wedding date was unknown.

One morning Rosamond's aunt came to visit her. Mrs Bulstrode, married to the town's banker, was Mr Vincy's sister. She had disapproved of her brother's choice of wife – and her husband, who knew the financial history of everyone in Middlemarch, disapproved of the Vincys' attitude to money. The children had no idea of saving, believing that their father had a bottomless pocket and could pay for anything if he chose. Mr Vincy himself had expensive habits, spending money on horses, wine and dinner parties, while Mrs Vincy bought what she wanted without asking the price. But Mrs Bulstrode was a kind woman and very fond of her niece. On this occasion, an alarming piece of news had just reached her – that Rosamond was engaged to Mr Lydgate.

'Why has your father not told me this news, Rosamond?' said Mrs Bulstrode, as they sat alone in the sitting room.

'I am not engaged, aunt,' said Rosamond, her face a deep red.

'They why is everyone saying so?'

'I am not interested in what "everyone" says,' said Rosamond, secretly pleased.

'Oh, my dear,' said Mrs Bulstrode. 'Remember that you are now twenty-two, and you have no fortune. Your father won't be able to give you anything. Mr Lydgate is clever and your uncle Bulstrode finds him very useful. But doctors are not well paid and you won't like being married to a poor man.'

'My Lydgate *isn't* a poor man, Aunt,' said Rosamond. 'He has fine relations; there is a baronet in his family.'

'He told me himself that he is poor,' said Mrs Bulstrode. 'Has he made an offer to you?'

Poor Rosamond's pride was hurt. The truth was, he had not asked her. She chose to be silent.

'Then he is playing with your love,' said Mrs Bulstrode. 'There are other young men in Middlemarch. Ned Plymdale is a nice young man, and people say he is good-looking. He may not be as clever as Mr Lydgate, but he has a successful business and is rich.'

'I have already refused Ned Plymdale,' said Rosamond. 'If I marry, it will be for love.' Rosamond felt that she played the part of a romantic heroine prettily.

Mrs Bulstrode decided that she must act, and arranged a meeting with the young doctor. After discussing Fred Vincy's health, she turned to the dangers facing young people today.

'A gentleman, for example,' said Mrs Bulstrode, 'may pretend to be in love with a young lady for his own amusement. But while he is enjoying himself, he may drive away other men who might make an offer to the young lady. Mr Lydgate, you know that our young men can't compete with you. Please don't spoil Rosamond's chances of a good marriage.'

Lydgate was angry with himself; he had been behaving like a fool. He was sure that Rosamond herself was not serious about their relationship, but he decided that he would not go to Mr Vincy's house except on business.

Poor Rosamond became very unhappy. She did not see Lydgate for ten days, and she began to believe that he was playing with her feelings.

On the eleventh day, however, Lydgate visited Fred Vincy and his mother at Uncle Featherstone's in Lowick, where Fred was recovering from his fever, away from the unhealthy air of the manufacturing town and close to the dying old man. As Lydgate was leaving Stone Court, Mrs Vincy asked him to give her husband a message. Instead of leaving it at the door, Lydgate decided to have a few sweet words with Rosamond – to laugh at the Middlemarchers' idea that a conversation or two between a man and a woman always resulted in a wedding.

Miss Vincy was alone, reading. Her face became so red when Lydgate came into the room that he, too, was embarrassed. The playful words he had planned went out of his head, and he formally gave his message from Mrs Vincy without smiling. Rosamond, who had felt her happiness returning at the sight of him, thanked him coldly, returning to her book. Lydgate sat silently but could say nothing; the loudest noise in the room was the clock. He suddenly stood up, and Rosamond dropped her book. Lydgate bent down to pick it up. As he stood up again, he saw tears pouring down Rosamond's beautiful cheeks.

'What is the matter?' said Lydgate.

Rosamond could not speak, and Lydgate realised that this lovely creature depended on him for her happiness. He put his arms around her gently, and kissed her tears. When he left the house half an hour later, Lydgate was engaged.

◆

It was a May morning when old Mr Featherstone was buried in Lowick churchyard. He had been a wealthy man, who had used his money to exercise power over his many poorer relatives. They were all there now, gathered around his grave, hoping that he had remembered them in his will. But Mr Featherstone continued to play cruel games with his relatives even after death.

The little church could be seen from Lowick Manor, and a group watched from a window there, including Dorothea, her uncle, Celia and her new husband Sir James, and Mrs Cadwallader, a neighbour. Mr Casaubon sat a little apart from them, reading.

'Who are they all?' asked Celia, as people came out of the church.

'Some of them are Lowick farmers and Featherstone's tenants,' said Sir James, 'but most must be Featherstone relatives.'

'There is Mr Vincy,' said Mr Brooke, 'I believe his boy Fred is likely to inherit the land and the house.'

'Who is that strange little man standing apart from the rest,' asked Mrs Cadwallader, 'the one with the frog face?'

'Oh yes! What an odd face!' said Celia. 'And look over there! Dorothea, you never told me that Mr Ladislaw was in Lowick.'

Everyone noticed the shock in Dorothea's face; she looked at her uncle, while Mr Casaubon looked at her.

'Who is *he*?' asked Mrs Cadwallader, wondering at the meaning behind the looks in the room.

'He is a young relative of Mr Casaubon's,' said Sir James.

'He is nice-looking, don't you think?' said Celia.

'He came here with me,' said Mr Brooke, smiling at

Dorothea. 'He is my guest at Tipton Grange, and he has brought the painting from Rome. You know, Casaubon, the picture with you as Thomas Aquinas. It is in my carriage. The painter has captured your features exactly. Young Ladislaw is good company. I hope he will stay with me a long time. I have plenty of ideas and facts, you know, and he is the right man to organise them for me. I invited him when you were ill, Casaubon. Dorothea said you couldn't have anybody in the house, and she asked me to write to him.'

Mr Casaubon smiled with cold politeness at Mr Brooke, but said nothing. He guessed that Dorothea had asked her uncle to invite Will to Tipton Grange, and poor Dorothea felt unable to explain in front of their guests.

'He has a good future ahead of him,' said Mr Brooke. 'He will make me a good secretary. I shall go and fetch him.'

As Mr Featherstone's family gathered at Stone Court for the reading of his will, the frog-faced stranger among them was causing alarm. His name was Joshua Rigg, but nobody knew who he was.

Fred Vincy, however, whom everyone expected to inherit Stone Court, was not alarmed and was trying not to laugh. The relatives formed a ridiculous group, each believing his or her own claim on the old man's money to be fair, while unimpressed by the expectations of more distant cousins. As the lawyer entered the room, with papers in his hand, the room fell silent.

Mr Featherstone had always planned to reach his dead hand out from his grave to shock his relatives. The lawyer read out the will, which left ten thousand pounds to Fred Vincy and small amounts to each of his relatives. Fred smiled and the relatives expressed their disgust. The lawyer coughed and everyone fell silent again.

'There is a second will,' he said. 'It is dated a year later, and so we may throw the first will on the fire.'

As the lawyer read out the details, the smile left Fred's face. He and the other relatives would inherit nothing. Everything – house, money, land – was left instead to Mr Joshua Rigg.

'Who is he?' demanded the relatives, all talking at once.

'He is Mr Featherstone's son,' said the lawyer, silencing the room again. 'Mr Featherstone wasn't married to Mr Rigg's mother, but he wished at the end of his life to recognise Joshua as his son.'

Mr Vincy went home from the reading of the will in a very bad mood. His lazy son Fred had no fortune now, so he saw Rosamond's engagement to Lydgate in a different light.

'I can't afford to pay for the wedding,' he said.

'But Rosamond has chosen her wedding dress,' said Mrs Vincy.

'Business is bad. Lydgate has little income and plenty of enemies. Why did we give Rosamond such an expensive education, if she then marries a poor man? The engagement is at an end; I won't agree to it and you'd better tell your daughter.'

Rosamond remained quite calm as her mother gave her this news.

'Papa doesn't mean it,' she said. 'He has always said that I must marry the man I love. And I shall marry Mr Lydgate. It is seven weeks now since papa agreed to our marriage. And I have seen a house I like – Lowick Gate.'

'Lowick Gate is very large, dear. It will need a lot of furniture and carpets. Do you think Mr Lydgate can afford it?'

'I am not going to ask him that, Mamma!'

'But your father can't give you any money, my dear, and Fred has nothing from Mr Featherstone –'

'That has nothing to do with my marriage, Mamma. Fred must find a job.' And Rosamond went out to visit the dress-maker.

In fact, Mr Vincy could never say no to his darling daughter, and she soon persuaded him not to change his mind.

He made it clear to her, however, that although he would pay for the wedding, he would not give them any money for furniture.

'I have nothing to spare,' he said. 'So please tell your husband not to expect anything.'

But Rosamond never paid attention to financial matters. She said nothing to Lydgate, and soon forgot that the conversation had ever happened.

Lydgate wanted to marry as soon as possible, because Rosamond expected him to visit the Vincy house every evening. This interrupted his studies and upset his sense of his own social position; Mr and Mrs Vincy were from a lower social class, and he did not enjoy their company. He wished to become master of his time again. So he rented the Lowick Gate house that Rosamond liked, and asked her to agree a date.

'Let us marry in six weeks' time, my love,' he said one evening when they were alone. 'I am sure you won't mind about new clothes. They can be bought afterwards.'

'What strange ideas you clever men have,' laughed Rosamond. 'I have never heard of wedding clothes being bought after a wedding. And there are curtains, plates and furniture to be arranged for the house. But I am sure my mother could look after that while we are away.'

'Yes, of course. We must be away for a week or two.'

'Oh, longer than that!' said Rosamond.

Lydgate imagined that she wanted to spend more time alone with him. In fact, she was hoping to spend at least part of the honeymoon at the home of his uncle, Sir Godwin Lydgate, the baronet.

Lydgate was no better with money than his future wife. One day, for example, he saw a set of dinner plates in a shop window that looked exactly right and bought them at once. They were expensive, but Lydgate hated things that were ugly or of poor quality. When he first came to Middlemarch, he had bought Dr Peacock's practice, which left him with eight hundred pounds in the bank. He had gained some new patients, but lost others, and his income was not as much as he had expected. His eight hundred pounds was now greatly reduced, but of course Mr Vincy would give them money when they married towards their new home, as fathers always did. He had not discussed the amount with Mr Vincy, but Lydgate guessed it would be a few hundred pounds. He would use that to pay the bills from the furniture shops.

'I do want to meet your family,' said Rosamond one day. 'You were often at Sir Godwin's house when you were a boy, weren't you? I would love to see where you played as a child. Does Sir Godwin know that you are getting married?'

'No,' said Lydgate carelessly. 'But I will write to him if you like. My cousins are such bores, though.'

The idea of speaking about a baronet's family as 'bores' was wonderful to Rosamond, and she felt that nothing could spoil her future happiness.

Chapter 4   Politics, Prison and Poison

The latest news in the pubs, dining rooms and kitchens of Middlemarch was that Mr Brooke of Tipton Grange had secretly bought the *Pioneer*, one of the town's two newspapers, and that he had employed a young man with foreign blood, a Mr Will Ladislaw, to write it for him. Mr Brooke was a supporter of progress and reform – if the progress and reform was taking place in other parts of England, not at Tipton Grange – and it was clear that he intended to stand for Parliament.

'Young Ladislaw can understand any political situation,'

Mr Brooke explained to Mr Casaubon one afternoon. 'He can add facts from memory, and ideas, and that sort of thing, and write about it in an excellent piece for the paper. He loves independence and freedom – fine feelings, you know. I think I can start him on a good career.'

Mr Casaubon had disliked Will when he was paying for his education; he disliked him even more now that he was not. He guessed that Will laughed at him, and now the young man was free to laugh even more loudly. On his side, Will had been sincerely grateful to Mr Casaubon in the past, but he could not forgive him for marrying Dorothea. A man may choose to live like a ghost in a cave, but he had no right to capture a young girl and pull her in with him.

Will received no formal invitations to Lowick, but Mr Brooke was unaware of Mr Casaubon's feelings about his cousin, and often brought Will with him on his visits. Dorothea always enjoyed their conversations. Before her marriage, she had never met anyone who was interested in the same things as her – and since her marriage, she had not enjoyed her husband's superior intelligence as much as she had expected. If she expressed a new idea to Mr Casaubon, he listened patiently and then referred to a historical person who had had a similar hopeless idea; or he would simply say that she was mistaken. When she saw Will, a window opened temporarily in her prison wall, allowing her to smell the fresh air for a moment. Because Mr Casaubon had said nothing about Will's arrival at Tipton Grange, she now innocently hoped that they could all be friends.

Will was waiting impatiently for an opportunity to talk to Dorothea alone. He knew where she walked each morning in the grounds of Lowick Manor, and one day he took paper and pencil there, sat down under a tree and began to draw. But it started to rain heavily, so he ran to the house and knocked on the door. Mr Casaubon's servant answered.

'Please don't interrupt Mr Casaubon,' Will said. 'I know he is working. I shall wait in the sitting room until lunchtime.'

'Mr Casaubon is out, sir,' said the servant. 'I will tell Mrs Casaubon you are here.'

'Oh, very well,' said Will, hiding his delight. 'This rotten rain has stopped me from drawing.'

Dorothea met him with her sweet smile. Wearing a plain white dress and no jewellery except her wedding ring, she explained that Mr Casaubon was away until dinner.

'I really wanted to see you alone,' said Will. 'To talk as we did in Rome, about art and life. It never seems to be the same when there are other people here.'

They sat opposite each other, like two flowers that had just opened in the morning sunshine.

'I have learnt a little Latin since we were in Rome,' said Dorothea. 'And some Greek too. I can help Mr Casaubon better now, finding particular notes for him and saving his eyes. People seem to get so tired on their way to great thoughts.'

'If a man is going to have great thoughts, he usually has them when he is still young,' said Will quickly. But he saw Dorothea's face change, and added immediately, 'But you are right, the best minds can easily get tired. And, he has shown justice to me in family matters, by paying for my education. It was terrible that my grandmother was disinherited because of her marriage. And there was nothing wrong with her husband except that he had escaped trouble in Poland and worked as a teacher.'

'I would like to know all about her,' said Dorothea. 'She gave up her wealth for love. Was her life happy?'

'I know little about my grandparents – only that my grandfather spoke many languages and was musical. They both died young, like my father. I remember my father's last illness, when I was about four. We were very hungry, with only bread to eat.'

'What a different life from mine!' said Dorothea. 'And Mr Casaubon didn't know about you at that time.'

'No. When my father made contact with Mr Casaubon, that was my last hungry day. My father died soon after that, and Mr Casaubon took care of my mother and me. He knew it was his duty, because my grandmother had been so badly treated.'

Will wanted to make it clear to Dorothea that Mr Casaubon was simply paying a debt.

'He has never told me that he supported your mother,' she said. 'Is she still alive?'

'No, she died in an accident four years ago. It is strange that my mother, too, ran away from her family – but not because of a husband. There was a reason why she couldn't stay with her family, but she never told me what it was. She went on the stage to support herself. You see, I come from rebel blood on both sides!'

'That explains why you haven't followed Mr Casaubon's advice,' smiled Dorothea. 'And if he seems to dislike you, remember that his studies have made him sensitive. And he has been ill.'

Will realised that Dorothea's feelings towards her husband were pity and loyalty but not love, and he was truly happy. 'I will never again do or say anything that you would disapprove of,' he said.

'That is very good of you,' laughed Dorothea. 'But I expect you will leave us soon. Are you tired of staying with my uncle?'

'Mr Brooke has asked me to stay,' said Will. 'He has bought the *Pioneer*, and now he has asked me to be the editor. Here is a chance for me to work at something. If you would prefer me not to accept, I will give it up. But I would like to stay in this part of the country.'

'And I would like you to stay very much,' said Dorothea, as simply and openly as she had spoken in Rome. And then she added quickly, 'But perhaps my husband won't like the idea. Can you wait now and ask him?'

Will did not want to meet Mr Casaubon. He expected him to dislike the idea very much. 'No, I must go,' he said, jumping up. 'The rain has stopped now. I will walk back to Tipton Grange across the wet grass. I will enjoy that.'

It was four o'clock before Mr Casaubon returned from his meeting in Brassing. He was unusually cheerful.

'I met Dr Spanning today, and he spoke very admiringly of my recent report on the Egyptian myths. I won't repeat what he said,' said Mr Casaubon, trying to hide a smile.

'I am very glad,' said Dorothea. And then she told her husband about Will's visit. She explained her uncle's offer to Will, and then asked what Mr Casaubon's opinion was. He looked at Dorothea through narrow eyes and was silent.

'I feared you might object,' she said. 'But such a talented man will be useful to my uncle, and you want him to find a profession.'

Again he did not answer, and when she referred to Dr Spanning's remarks, the sunshine was gone from his face.

The next morning, Mr Casaubon wrote to Will. 'Dear Mr Ladislaw, Your acceptance of Mr Brooke's offer would be highly offensive to me,' he wrote. 'Although you are not now receiving financial support from me, you have in the past, and I believe this gives me a right to express an opinion on this matter. I do not wish a cousin of mine to take such a low job with my wife's uncle, and within five miles of my home. If you decide to take the post, you will not be welcome at my house.'

Dorothea knew nothing of this letter and was innocently thinking of Will's grandmother, cut off from her family because she married a poor man. What injustice! She thought of her husband's will, which left all his money and property to her. Surely here was a chance for her husband to repay fully the debt to the Ladislaws. If her husband disapproved of Mr Brooke's offer to Will, and she was sure he would, why did he not pay Will a regular income during his life, and leave Will a large share of his money when he died?

'I am sure he will agree with me,' she thought. 'We make no use of half our income.' She chose a quiet moment to open the subject with her husband. As usual, and as Celia had often warned her, she was blind to what was obvious to others. They sat beside the fire, and darkness fell outside as she explained her idea.

'Mr Ladislaw has been speaking to you about this, I imagine,' Mr Casaubon said bitterly.

'No,' said Dorothea. 'How can you imagine that? You are too critical of him, my dear. He only told me a little about his family, and all in answer to my questions. You have been so good, so just to him, but it seems to me that it is right to do more.'

'Dorothea, my love,' said Mr Casaubon, 'this is not the first time that you have given an opinion on a subject of which you know nothing. You have no right to come between me and Mr Ladislaw, and especially not to discuss my affairs with him.'

The fire had burnt down now and poor Dorothea was in a storm of emotions. She said nothing because she had heard her husband's anger and was frightened that his heart would suddenly fail again. But her soul cried silently for help in bearing this life in which all her dreams and ideas were killed by her husband's disapproval and her fear for his health.

The next morning, Mr Casaubon received a reply to his letter.

'Dear Mr Casaubon, I will always be grateful for your generous help to me in the past. That help, however, does not give you the right to tell me where to live or what profession to follow. My acceptance of Mr Brooke's offer will have no effect on you or your position at Lowick. Yours sincerely, Will Ladislaw.'

Mr Casaubon was disgusted. Will was obviously in Middlemarch because of Dorothea. Why else had he suddenly refused financial help and returned to England? Mr Casaubon did not suspect Dorothea for one second, but he thought that Will had power over her opinions, especially about her husband. He continued to believe that Dorothea had asked Mr Brooke to invite Will to Tipton Grange, and he was too proud to question her about this directly.

'I cannot speak to Brooke or Sir James,' he thought. 'They will suspect I am jealous, and say I was wrong to marry Dorothea.'

And so he remained silent. But although he had lost this battle with Will, the war between them had not ended. He had other weapons.

♦

The more Mr Brooke liked the idea of standing for Parliament, the more anxious Sir James became. Although he knew very little about politics, Sir James felt that Mr Brooke knew even less. He wanted to protect his wife's uncle from making a fool of himself.

As they sat together after dinner at Freshitt Hall one evening, Sir James introduced the subject.

'Have you read this piece in the newspaper about "a landowner not far from Middlemarch"? It means you, Brooke. It says you are kind-hearted to factory workers in the cities, while your own tenants are hungry and the gates to all your fields are falling to pieces.'

'Oh, that stupid reporter at the *Trumpet*,' said Brooke.

'There isn't a word of truth in what he writes.'

'He is right about the repairs, Brooke,' said Sir James. 'One of your tenants complained to me the other day that rain was coming through his roof. You ought to repair it.'

'I know you spend a lot of money on your farm, Sir James,' said Mr Brooke. 'It is your hobby, and you don't mind doing that.'

'If you want people to vote for you,' said Sir James, annoyed now, 'you must make sure your business is well run. You need an estate manager who will take care of repairs and charge fair rents.'

Sir James's anxiety about Brooke was now greater than before their conversation. He decided to take advantage of Mr Brooke's affection for Dorothea, and wrote to her about the problems on the Tipton Grange farms.

Dorothea arrived at her uncle's home a few days later, while Will and Mr Brooke were working in the library. Will jumped up; it seemed that an electric shock had passed through his body.

'Sir James has been telling me of your plans for Tipton,' Dorothea said to her uncle. 'You are going to employ an estate manager.'

'Yes, well, I never said I would or I wouldn't do that, my dear,' said Mr Brooke.

'He is confident that you *will* do it,' said Dorothea clearly, 'because you wish to enter Parliament as a member who cares about reform. And the best place to start is at Tipton. Think of the Dagley family, with the roof falling in on their old farmhouse, who live in the back kitchen and leave the other rooms to the rats! We can't argue for a better world until we make improvements on our own doorstep.'

This was the first time since her marriage that Dorothea had been able to pour out her feelings. Will stared at her in admiration, while Mr Brooke did not know where to look.

At that moment a servant came in with a dead rabbit in one

hand and the ear of one of the young Dagley boys in the other.

'I am coming,' said Mr Brooke cheerfully, grateful to the Dagley boy for providing a means of escape. 'I shall be very kind to him,' he said to Dorothea, 'very kind.'

'I hope you agree with me,' said Dorothea to Will, as soon as her uncle had gone.

'Yes, now I have heard you speak about it,' said Will. 'I shall not forget your words. But can I ask you about another matter?'

'Of course,' said Dorothea.

'You know that Mr Casaubon has forbidden me to visit Lowick? He hates my position here, but I think his attitude is ridiculous. I believe I can do a useful job here and remain a gentleman.'

'I didn't know about this,' said Dorothea, clearly upset.

'I shall never see you now,' said Will. 'I won't hear your news.'

'There *is* no news,' said Dorothea. 'I am always at Lowick.'

'Your life there is like a prison,' said Will angrily.

'No. I have a way to live. I believe that we must always try to do good, even when our path isn't clear. In that way, the world becomes a better place. What helps *you* most with life?'

'I love to see goodness and beauty,' said Will. 'But I am a rebel – I wouldn't live a life that I didn't like, as you do.'

'My uncle is a long time,' said Dorothea, feeling that she could not continue this conversation. 'I must find him and go to Freshitt Hall – Celia is expecting me. She is so happy there with Sir James. It is a pleasure to visit.'

Mr Brooke was just returning from the Dagleys' cottage when Dorothea went outside to her carriage. His face was red and he looked upset. Dagley had not been impressed by Mr Brooke's kindness to his boy about the stolen rabbit; large quantities of beer had given him the confidence to accuse Mr Brooke loudly and offensively of being mean. Mr Brooke had never been insulted by one of his tenants before, and had believed himself to be popular.

The comments in the *Trumpet*, the arguments of Sir James and then Dorothea, and now a drunk Dagley finally had an effect on Mr Brooke. The following week a letter arrived on the kitchen table of Caleb Garth, Sir James's estate manager, asking him to manage Tipton Grange as well as Freshitt Hall. Caleb started work at once, writing new agreements with the tenants, beginning repairs to their cottages and introducing new ideas for farming.

Caleb received two other letters at the same time as Mr Brooke's offer of work. One was from Joshua Rigg and the other was from Mr Bulstrode, but both letters asked him to value Stone Court and its land, old Mr Featherstone's estate.

While Caleb was opening his letters, Joshua Rigg was standing at the window of Stone Court, looking out. 'Frog-faced' Rigg was neat and well-dressed, but a second person in the room was untidy and red-faced. His name was John Raffles, and the nasty smell of cheap hotels hung around him. Raffles was Rigg's stepfather, and he was now trying to try to persuade Rigg to share his inheritance.

'Listen to me,' said Rigg quietly, without looking away from the window, after Raffles had described his plan to open a tobacco shop. 'You kicked me when I was a boy; you ate the best food in the house, leaving none for me and my mother; you stole our possessions and sold them to buy drink. Now you expect me to give you money! I shall give my mother money each week, direct to her, and that is all. Now go.'

As he always did when he was losing a game, Raffles took a small bottle of alcohol from his pocket and drank it all.

'All right, Joshua, my boy,' he said, smiling. 'Fill my bottle and give me a gold coin, and I'll go. I'll go like a bullet!'

Rigg handed Raffles a few coins. As his stepson was

48

unlocking his drinks cupboard, Raffles picked up a part-burned piece of paper from the fireplace. He wrapped the coins in it and pushed it into his pocket.

Rigg did not speak another word to his stepfather, but watched him leave the grounds of Stone Court. He never saw him again.

♦

One of Lydgate's first professional calls after his return from his honeymoon was to Mr Casaubon, who wanted an honest opinion about the state of his health. Mr Casaubon had fully recovered his ability to work, and the attack had perhaps been the result of tiredness. He hoped he had twenty years of great writing ahead of him, so he had not wasted the thirty years of preparation. But perhaps the illness was deep at work inside him, and his life might end much sooner. The thought that Will Ladislaw would enter his nest if he died was like a poison eating his body.

When Lydgate arrived at Lowick, he joined Mr Casaubon on his daily walk in the garden. Newly married and full of young energy himself, Lydgate was shocked by his patient's aged appearance.

'You are suffering from a type of heart disease,' Lydgate explained. 'You might live a comfortable life for another fifteen years. But I must tell you that it can strike you dead at any time.'

Mr Casaubon thanked Lydgate for his plain speaking, and the doctor left him. People often say, 'We must all die.' To Mr Casaubon, that had suddenly become, 'I must die – and soon.' With his head bent forward, he continued to walk under the darkening trees, feeling the cruel fingers of death around his neck.

When Dorothea came to find him in the garden, worried that Lydgate's words had upset him, he looked coldly at her.

When she put her arm through his, he did not smile. When they reached the house, he did not speak. He went into the library and shut the door.

Dorothea ran up to her little sitting room and threw herself in a chair. Tears did not come. Instead there was anger.

'What have I done? Why does he treat me like this?'

She understood that there was no emotional connection between them, and that was the problem. He gave her no chance to share his life. 'It is *his* fault, not mine,' she thought bitterly. Her servant came into the room to say that Mr Casaubon wished to have dinner alone in the library. Dorothea refused dinner herself and sent her servant away.

As evening turned to night, her anger melted and she began to feel sorry for her husband; the knowledge that he could never complete his life's work must be breaking his heart. At ten o'clock, the time when Mr Casaubon usually came to bed, Dorothea went to the top of the stairs and waited in the darkness. She heard the library door open, and watched her husband climb the stairs.

'Dorothea!' he said gently. 'Are you waiting for me?'

She smiled warmly, put her hand into her husband's, and they walked along to the bedroom together.

Chapter 5   The Dead Hand

Two days later Dorothea drove into Middlemarch. She told her husband that she had some shopping to do, but actually hoped to speak to Lydgate about Mr Casaubon's health. Since the doctor's visit, Mr Casaubon had begun a new method of arranging his notes, and he was now involving Dorothea in the work.

Lydgate was out, but his wife was at home. As Dorothea waited in the hall, she heard a few notes of a piano and a man's voice coming from the sitting room. The voice sounded familiar to her.

The music stopped suddenly and Dorothea was shown in. The two people in the room had jumped to their feet when Mrs Casaubon's name was announced. One was Rosamond, who had received high praise at Sir Godwin Lydgate's home on her recent honeymoon, and who now felt she had stepped into Dorothea's social class. Rosamond was also delighted to give Mrs Casaubon an opportunity to study *her*; what is the point of looking beautiful if you are not seen by the best judges?

'I am so sorry to interrupt you, Mrs Lydgate,' said Dorothea. 'I am anxious to see Mr Lydgate. May I wait for him?'

'He is at the new hospital,' said Rosamond. 'I can send for him, Mrs Casaubon.'

The other person in the room, who now stepped forward, was Will Ladislaw, looking rather embarrassed.

'I didn't expect to see you here,' Dorothea said, holding out her hand and smiling with unmistakable pleasure. Then she had a sudden thought, and became hardly conscious of her actions. Why was Will here alone with Rosamond?

'I will go to the hospital myself, Mrs Lydgate,' she said. 'Please excuse me,' and she went out to her carriage.

During the short journey to the hospital, Dorothea replayed the scene in Mrs Lydgate's sitting room in her head. It was strange that Will was spending time with Mr Lydgate's wife while Lydgate himself was out! Did Mr Lydgate know? Tears came, and she did not really know why, because she had no idea that she was beginning to fall in love with Will. She only knew that her feelings towards Will had been spoiled by the short visit.

Will was very annoyed. The history of the scene that Dorothea had walked into was simple. There were few interesting people in Middlemarch, and Lydgate was one of them. He also had a wife who was pleasant and musical. Will did not care about the rules of society; he knew that he always behaved like a perfect gentleman. But how had it looked to Dorothea?

'Mrs Casaubon looks very clever,' said Rosamond. 'Is she?'

'I have never thought about it,' said Will unhappily.

'That is just what my husband said,' replied Rosamond. 'What are you men thinking of when you are with Mrs Casaubon?'

'When one sees a perfect woman,' said Will, 'one never thinks of her character – one feels her presence.'

Later, Rosamond described the afternoon to her husband, and stated that she believed Will was in love with Mrs Casaubon.

'Poor man!' said Lydgate with feeling. 'A man in love forgets about his work and spends money that he doesn't have.'

'I am sure *you* don't forget about your work. You are always at the hospital or seeing poor patients. And at home you are in your study looking at body parts in glass jars! You like your work better than me.'

'Don't you want your husband to be more than a Middlemarch doctor, Rosamond?' Lydgate asked. 'I must work hard if I want to have a reputation outside this town.'

'Of course I want you to make great discoveries, Tertius. But we cannot hide ourselves away. Are you unhappy with me?'

'No, my dear. I am completely happy.'

'What did Mrs Casaubon want to say to you?' Rosamond asked.

'She was worried about her husband's health. And she was very impressed with the new hospital: I think she will give us two hundred pounds a year! There is so much bad feeling towards Bulstrode in the town, and of course the doctors see me as an enemy, so help from someone like Mrs Casaubon is very useful.'

When Mr Farebrother visited later that evening, Lydgate was feeling cheerful. They discussed the refusal of all the Middlemarch doctors to use the new hospital.

'They will not drive me away,' Lydgate said. 'I can earn enough for our needs now that the wedding is behind us and Rosamond and I are happily settled in our own home.'

'I have two pieces of advice,' said the friendly clergyman. 'Don't get too close to Bulstrode and be careful about money. I know you disapprove of my betting, and you are right, so don't spend money that you haven't got.'

'I don't care about Bulstrode, except for the money that he puts into the hospital,' replied Lydgate. 'But I note your advice about money. I have made a few small debts recently.'

Lydgate stretched out comfortably on the sofa, chatting with his friend while Rosamond played the piano, and thinking that life was quite good. It was not *very* good, because that day he had received a letter demanding immediate payment for the furniture. He said nothing to Rosamond; she was expecting a baby and he did not want to worry her.

♦

Will Ladislaw discovered that the world of politics suited the rebel inside him. He was conscious that he spoke well in public and wrote well, and he found himself more enthusiastic about the political situation than he had ever been about poetry or painting. Although he often lost his patience with Mr Brooke's half-hearted support for political reform and wandering mind, he enjoyed Middlemarch life.

There were many things against him in the town's opinion: he was too clever, he had a Polish parent, and he mixed freely with the lowest people in society. It was even said he sometimes lay full length on the carpet in front of other people's fires while he talked. People might behave like that in free-thinking London houses, but they certainly did not in Middlemarch. He was in fact welcome in several homes: the Bulstrode house, where reforming ideas were popular; the Farebrother house, where he was a favourite with the ladies, and the Lydgate house, where his singing and interesting conversation were admired.

Mr Casaubon was wrong to suspect Will of plotting to marry Dorothea after his death in order to get Mr Casaubon's money. Will loved Dorothea with his whole being, but he did not imagine that Dorothea would ever love him. He knew that she liked him, and he believed that in other circumstances she could love him, but she was not free to love, and that was the end of it. So why did he stay in Middlemarch? She had once said she would like him to stay, and therefore he would stay, even if he could only admire her from a distance.

♦

'Before I sleep,' said Mr Casaubon to his wife one night as they got into bed, 'I have a request to make, Dorothea. Please let me know that if I die you will obey my wishes. Will you do as I ask?'

Dorothea did not answer immediately.

'Do you refuse?' he asked anxiously.

'No, I don't yet refuse,' said Dorothea, in a clear voice, 'but I can't promise when I don't know what you want me to do. Can you wait until tomorrow?'

'Until tomorrow then,' said Mr Casaubon.

While her husband slept, Dorothea imagined the months and years ahead of her, sorting through his dusty notes to produce a work of doubtful value. She had married him to help with his life's work, when she had thought the work was something greater. If he lived for fifteen more years, she would spend her life helping him and obeying him. She lay awake half the night, feeling ill and helpless.

As she went downstairs to breakfast the next morning, she had made up her mind to give him the answer that he wanted.

'I am not feeling well, my dear,' said Mr Casaubon when he saw her. 'I am going out to walk in the garden. What is your answer?'

'May I come out to the garden soon, my dear,' she said.

'I will wait for you there,' he said.

Dorothea drank a cup of tea, but could not eat breakfast. She sat quietly, thinking of the living hell that lay before her, knowing she was too weak to refuse. She would promise, and then she would have to keep her promise. Finally, she went out into the garden. Her husband sat at a stone table, his head resting on his arms.

'Look how tired he is,' she thought. 'I am here, Edward,' she said, sitting down next to him. 'I am ready to promise.'

She tried to wake him from his sleep, but he did not move.

'Edward! Edward!' she cried, shaking him.

But it was too late. Mr Casaubon was dead.

For the next few days, Dorothea stayed with Celia and Sir James, and their new baby boy, at Freshitt Hall, so she did not learn immediately what was in her husband's will. But after a week of sitting sadly while Celia played with the baby, she felt ready to visit Lowick Manor, and to decide what to do with her money. She also needed to appoint a new clergyman for Lowick Church. Sir James drove her home, and left her to look through her husband's papers.

Her eyes ran over Mr Casaubon's will. He had left Lowick Manor and its land to her as expected. But then her blood ran cold. He had recently added a sentence at the bottom. As she read his spidery writing, a knife seemed to twist in her heart: 'If Dorothea ever marries Mr Will Ladislaw, she must leave

Lowick Manor immediately. She will lose the house, the land and the income.'

Everything in Dorothea's life took on a new form at that moment: her husband's behaviour, her own feelings and her relationship with Will. She suddenly saw her husband's hidden thoughts, and they shocked her violently. At the same time, she felt a great wave of feeling towards Will. It had never entered her mind that he might love her, or that Mr Casaubon or Will himself had ever imagined it. She knew that her uncle and Sir James had already seen the will. What must they think?

She returned to Freshitt Hall with various business papers. She put her husband's meanness out of her mind, anxious to begin performing her duties as the new owner of Lowick Manor. When Lydgate visited, she mentioned her search for a new clergyman. Lydgate suggested Mr Farebrother, hoping that he could make a past wrong right.

'Farebrother's mother, aunt and sister all live with him,' explained Lydgate. 'They depend on him. I believe he has never married because of them. And he preaches very well in church – his ideas are original and his words are clear. He has little money, however, and that has led him to betting on card games, but he is one of the most honest men I have ever met.'

'Would he like to give up his card-playing habit?' asked Dorothea.

'Definitely,' said Lydgate. 'He would be glad of the time to follow his scientific interests. He knows all about insects.'

This was just what Dorothea liked – an opportunity to rescue a man. She decided to listen to Mr Farebrother preach.

♦

Although Mr Brooke continued to employ Will as editor of the *Pioneer* and as his election manager, he invited him less often to Tipton Grange. This was mainly to please Sir James, who hated Will's political views and had a very low opinion of him generally, especially after the mention of him in Mr Casaubon's will.

Will felt that the distance between himself and Dorothea was almost impossible to bridge. If he wanted to win her, he must make his fortune first. He did not know about the will, but he would not allow people to think that he wished to marry a rich widow for her money. He thought of leaving; if he showed any interest in Dorothea, people would try to poison her against him. But he could not leave Mr Brooke just before the election. Mr Brooke would not win unless Will persuaded more voters to support his reform ideas. And Mr Brooke did his best to confuse voters by always agreeing with the argument he had last heard. Will had written many speeches for his employer, but the older man's mind ran from one idea to another, often forgetting where it had started and having no idea where it was going.

One fine May morning, Mr Brooke prepared to make a speech to the people of Middlemarch. The town square was full and Mr Brooke was confident; he felt he had weakened the attacks of the *Trumpet* in the last six months by employing Caleb Garth to improve the tenants' lives on his estate.

He heard a few cheers as he climbed up onto a platform in front of his neighbours. 'Gentlemen of Middlemarch,' he began, 'I have never been so proud and happy in my life.' This fine opening to his speech was unfortunately not what he was supposed to say. Having taken the wrong road at the very beginning, his mind could not find its way back. He began to talk about everything and nothing, as he often did, and his unhappy listeners began to throw eggs at him.

Will was angry with himself as well as with Mr Brooke. He went back to his rooms thinking it was time to leave Middlemarch. Mr Brooke would surely give up politics now, so why should he stay? He must go away and make a success of his life somewhere else. In five years, he thought, he could make a reputation for political writing and political speaking, and then he could return and throw himself at Dorothea's feet. But he must be sure that she cared for him and that she knew his feelings for her.

His decision was made easier when he next met Mr Brooke.

'My heart is not strong enough,' said Mr Brooke, looking everywhere except at Will. 'Casaubon's death was a warning to me, you know. I must give up the election. And I am sure you are tired of this work, eh, Ladislaw? I have the highest opinion of your powers, but perhaps you are happy to give up the *Pioneer*?'

Realising at once that Dorothea's family had put pressure on Mr Brooke, Will felt himself rebelling. 'They have wanted him to get rid of me,' he said to himself, 'and now Brooke doesn't care if I go or stay. Well, I shall stay as long as I like. I shall go when I choose, and not because they don't like me.'

♦

Old Mr Featherstone, in his grave under the ground, would have been surprised to learn that Joshua Rigg, his long lost son, had no intention of living at Stone Court. Joshua Rigg had always wanted to be a money changer with a small shop, and so he sold Stone Court to Mr Bulstrode.

Mr Bulstrode rode there almost daily, looking forward to the time when he would retire from the bank. He did not deny to himself that there were mistakes in his past, but twenty years of a strictly moral life had surely repaid his debt to God.

One summer's evening, he was sitting on his horse admiring the house from the road, when a figure in black appeared and called to him.

'Hello, Nick! It's you, if I'm not mistaken, although it's twenty-five years since I last saw you. You didn't expect to see me here, eh!'

Even in the dying sun, it was clear that Mr Bulstrode's usually pale face was now deathly white. A moment before, his past wrongdoing had been safely locked in his own heart, and now it stood in front of him in the shape of this hateful creature. Mr Bulstrode had climbed high in life, and had a long way to fall.

'No, I did *not* expect to see you here, Raffles,' he said.

'My stepson owns Stone Court,' said John Raffles proudly. 'I came to see him here once before. And I'm not surprised to see you; I picked up a letter from the fireplace on my last visit and when I opened it, there was your name on it! I don't care about seeing my stepson; he's a cruel boy, and his poor mother's dead now. I came for *your* address, Nick.'

'Mr Rigg has gone,' said Bulstrode. 'I am master here now.'

'So you've left the old London business, and now you're a country gentleman. I expect your wife died a long time ago – gone to heaven without knowing how poor her daughter was, eh? I've kept that secret for you for a long time now. Perhaps you've married again, and there's a second Mrs Bulstrode. Ah! I see from your face that I'm right. Aren't you going to invite me in, Nick? I've walked for miles and I need a drink.'

Mr Bulstrode felt that he had little choice. Fortunately, he had continued to employ Joshua Rigg's housekeeper at Stone Court, and Mrs Abel would, he hoped, think that Raffles was a friend of her former employer. When food and drink were spread in front of Raffles, and they were alone, Mr Bulstrode spoke.

'I would like you, Raffles, to leave as soon as possible. Please explain why you wished to meet me. I imagine you have a home somewhere and will be glad to return to it.'

'I have no particular place to go, Nick.'

'Why did you return from America? You were given enough money to stay there for life.'

'I stayed for ten years. That was enough,' said Raffles.

'Do you wish to start a business? What is your profession now?'

'I don't care about work. I want enough money for a good life.'

'I can supply that if you agree to keep away from Middlemarch,' said the banker.

Raffles was enjoying Mr Bulstrode's discomfort. 'If I'd told the *first* Mrs Bulstrode that her daughter and grandson were alive,' he said, 'I'd have got more. But she's dead now. And you're rich, thanks to me. It's taken me a long time to find you, Nick.'

Mr Bulstrode had made up his mind. 'I am willing to supply you with payments every three months if you promise to keep away from Middlemarch. If you remain here, you will get nothing.'

'I don't want payments every three months! I like my freedom,' said Raffles. 'Give me two hundred, and I'll take my bag and go.'

'I have it here in the house,' said Mr Bulstrode, feeling suddenly pleased that Raffles might disappear, at least for now. He felt in this man's power, and he would do anything to escape from him.

'I didn't meet the old woman's daughter – Sarah,' said Raffles, taking the money. 'But I did find out her husband's name. I've forgotten it again now – it began with an "L".'

As Raffles was travelling away later that day, with Mr Bulstrode's two hundred pounds in his pocket, he suddenly said to himself, 'Ah! I remember. It was Ladislaw!'

Chapter 6   The Widow and the Wife

Dorothea stayed at Freshitt Hall for three months, until she could think of no new words of praise for Celia's baby, however perfect he was, and she returned to Lowick Manor.

She opened the curtains in the library, letting the sun fall on the rows of notebooks. She packed them all into a box and locked them away in a dark cupboard.

A deep desire had brought her back to Lowick; a desire to see Will. She knew that no good could come of their meeting, but her soul ached for him. Will was a favourite with the Farebrothers, who had moved to Lowick now that she had chosen Mr Farebrother as the new Lowick clergyman, and she was sure that Will would visit them. She often visited the Farebrother ladies, hoping for a mention of Will's name, but none was made.

One morning she sat in her little sitting room, looking at some papers, when her servant came in and announced that Mr Ladislaw was downstairs. At their first meeting in Rome, Dorothea had been calm and Will had been embarrassed. Now it was the other way around. Will knew nothing about Mr Casaubon's will, and could not understand why Dorothea seemed so uncomfortable with him.

'I hope you don't mind me visiting,' said Will. 'I couldn't bear to leave the neighbourhood without saying goodbye.'

'No – I hoped to see you,' said Dorothea. 'Are you going away immediately?'

'Very soon. I am going to study law, and then continue with political work. I hope I will make it my career.'

'You have so many talents,' said Dorothea, her embarrassment leaving her. She looked directly at Will, her eyes full of pleasure. 'My uncle says you speak well in public. When we were in Rome, I thought you cared only about art

61

and the pleasures of the rich, but now I know that you care about justice and the rest of the world.'

'So you approve of me going away for years,' said Will, 'and not returning until I have made my mark on the world?'

Dorothea looked out of the window at the rose bushes in the garden. How many times would they flower and die before Will came back? If he was going away, he must know about Mr Casaubon's will.

'You must do what you think is right,' she said. 'It will perhaps be a long time.' Will heard the tears behind her voice.

'I will never hear from you,' he said. 'You will forget me.'

'No,' said Dorothea, 'I shall never forget you.'

Will felt they were like two creatures turning to stone in each other's presence, while their hearts and their eyes were filled with desire. But he could not tell her how he felt; it would be like asking for her fortune. Her wealth and his poverty stood between them.

At that moment, the door opened and they turned away from each other. The servant announced Sir James, who hardly looked at Will – and Will hardly looked at him. Will said goodbye to Dorothea and left. They had needed five more minutes alone together, but now it was too late.

In the following days, Dorothea felt lost. Will was going away for years, and if he ever came back he would be another man. She took the little painting of his grandmother, so like him, from the wall and laid her cheek on it. She was beginning to realise that she was deeply in love.

♦

The arrival of Captain Lydgate, third son of Sir Godwin Lydgate, baronet, caused trouble at Lowick Gate. Rosamond was delighted with her guest; she felt herself floating above Middlemarch society, and forgot her growing disappointment with her marriage. Lydgate considered his cousin a fool, and rarely spoke to him.

Captain Lydgate had brought two horses with him. One was a gentle grey that he had bought for his sister and was taking back to Sir Godwin's. He begged Rosamond to try it for him, ignoring the fact that she was due to give birth in two months. Rosamond went out without telling her husband, and came back before his return. The ride was a great success, and she was sure Lydgate would be delighted.

Lydgate was, however, not happy. 'You have come back safely,' he said, 'but you mustn't go again, Rosy. Even on the quietest, most familiar horse in the world, there is always a chance of an accident.'

'There is the chance of an accident indoors,' said Rosamond.

'My darling, don't talk nonsense,' said Lydgate. 'It is enough that I say you mustn't ride again.'

But the pleasure of being seen on a fine horse with the son of a baronet at her side was too great for Rosamond. She did go again.

They rode along a path towards Lowick, with a wood on one side and a field on the other. A carriage was driving towards them, and Rosamond hoped it was one of Middlemarch's more important townspeople.

'Captain Lydgate, I think this horse will be perfect for your sister,' she said. 'I hope I will be able to see her riding very soon.'

'My dear Rosamond, I shall ask my sister to invite —'

There was a sudden crash as a tree fell to the ground in the wood. The gentle grey horse jumped sideways, badly frightened, and turned quickly, throwing Rosamond onto the grass at the side of the road.

At that moment the carriage reached them. Rosamond was lifted carefully inside and taken back to her house. Lydgate was called immediately. Rosamond was not badly hurt, but the baby could not be saved. Rosamond's greatest regret was that she never found out what the captain had intended to ask his sister.

Lydgate spoke tenderly to his wife and left her sleeping. Downstairs, he spoke very angrily to the Captain, who ordered his servant to pack his bags and left town the same evening.

Lydgate was secretly amazed at his powerlessness over Rosamond. She ignored his opinion on every practical question and simply did what she wanted. He was sure that they still loved each other, but they never seemed to be on the same mental path.

A dark shadow was growing over their lives, although Rosamond was completely unaware of it. Every day, they were getting deeper into debt. Their spending was increasing and their income was falling. Life in Middlemarch was less expensive than in London, but Lydgate felt that he had to keep two horses, he bought the best food and drink, and he paid a high rent for his house. Rosamond had learned her housekeeping skills from her mother and they consisted simply of ordering the best of everything.

Instead of trying to make a great discovery and improve human knowledge, Lydgate was forced to read unpleasant letters from tradesmen who wanted payment for furniture. He was too proud to ask Mr Vincy for help, and anyway he was aware that Mr Vincy's own affairs were in a bad state. He could not imagine borrowing from friends.

But when, some months later, Rosamond had regained her health, Lydgate decided to discuss his financial plans with his wife.

It was evening when he got home. Lydgate felt anxious as he asked his beautiful wife to come and sit beside him.

'Dear Rosy,' he said, 'I hate to say unpleasant things to you, but you must realise that we are short of money. We have a large debt of four hundred pounds. I have taken some financial advice, but we must decide together what to do about it.'

'What can *I* do, Tertius?' said Rosamond, looking at him in amazement. That short speech said so much, falling on Lydgate's soul like cold water.

'Some men – Dover's men – are coming to make a list of our furniture, plates, glasses and other possessions,' said Lydgate.

'Who is Dover?' asked Rosamond, colouring deeply.

'He lends money – and he can remove our possessions if we don't pay him back within an agreed time.'

Tears appeared in Rosamond's eyes. 'Haven't you asked papa for money?' she said, as soon as she could speak. 'I will ask him!'

'No, Rosy,' said Lydgate. He felt her tears like a knife in his heart. 'They are not taking the furniture yet; we can borrow money from Dover to pay our debt.'

Rosamond stood up and walked away from her husband.

'We have been spending too much for some time,' said Lydgate, 'but I didn't say anything and I am sorry. We must live more cheaply. I'm sure you will find all sorts of ways of saving money.'

'We could leave Middlemarch and sell everything,' said Rosamond, sitting down again. 'We could go to London, or to Durham, where your family is well known.'

'We can't go anywhere without money,' said Lydgate.

Rosamond was silent. She was asking herself why she had married a man who could behave like this.

'The jeweller is willing to take back some of our silver plates and jewellery. Here,' Lydgate said, showing her a list, 'I have marked some things that we could return to the shop.'

Rosamond left the room, leaving Lydgate helpless and wondering, but soon returned with her jewellery box. 'That is all the jewellery that you have ever given me,' she said coldly.

'Return whatever you please.'

'We must face this together, my darling,' said Lydgate. 'Please forgive me.' He was a warm-hearted man, and he felt he had failed as a husband.

◆

A few days later, Rosamond was entertaining Will Ladislaw. Her mood always improved in Will's company.

'I am not surprised you are still in Middlemarch,' she said playfully. 'Fred tells me that you have a beautiful reason to stay.'

'Nobody knows that better than you,' he said, trying to be polite.

'I mean, of course, Mrs Casaubon. The change that her husband made to his will to prevent her marrying you makes the situation even more romantic.'

'What do you mean?' said Will, beginning to shake violently. 'Don't joke; tell me what you mean.'

'You really don't know?' said Rosamond, seriously now. She explained everything that she had heard about Mr Casaubon's will: that if Dorothea married Will, she would lose Lowick Manor and her husband's money. 'But I am sure she likes you better than the house,' said Rosamond.

'Please don't say any more about it,' said Will, angrily. 'It is a horrible insult to her and to me.'

'I expect to hear of the marriage,' said Rosamond, smiling.

'You will never hear of the marriage!' said Will, and he left.

Poor Rosamond felt empty. Will did not care about her, Sir Godwin Lydgate's family never wrote to her, and Tertius talked only about money. She had already disobeyed her husband and asked her father for help, but Mr Vincy had refused, saying, 'I am likely to need help myself.'

Will still did not leave town, feeling that he must now

see Dorothea once more. One evening in the street, an unpleasant-looking man stepped in front of him.

'Excuse me, Mr Ladislaw,' said the man. 'Was your mother's name Sarah Dunkirk?'

'Yes, sir, it was,' said Will, stepping back from the stranger. 'And how is that your business?'

'I intend no offence, sir, no offence. But I knew your mother when she was a girl. My name's John Raffles, sir. I had the pleasure of meeting your father too, and you're very like him, Mr Ladislaw. Are your parents still alive?'

'No!' shouted Will, and stepped around Raffles and walked quickly away, but Raffles hurried to stay with him.

'I've often wondered what happened to your mother, sir,' said Raffles. 'She ran away from her friends when she was young – she had a proud spirit. I know the reason why she ran away.'

'Don't say anything to insult my mother,' said Will.

'I wouldn't, sir. She ran away because she was too honest. Her family were ... respectable thieves, sir. They had a fine shop, a high class pawnbroker's. But Sarah didn't like it – the possessions that people used for loans were often stolen, and no questions were asked. So she ran away from the business and the family. Look, sir, we're just passing a pub – shall we have a glass together?'

'No. I have nothing to say to you,' said Will, almost running to get away from Raffles. If Dorothea's friends knew this story, they would think him unfit to be in the same room as her. Well, they could think what they liked. His mother had managed to separate herself from her family, and had suffered great difficulties as a result, and her blood ran in his body.

Raffles decided to try his luck with his other 'friend' in Middlemarch, and presented himself at Mr Bulstrode's house. This time, Mr Bulstrode was able to send him away with twenty-five pounds, but the sight of Raffles at his door put the poor banker into a state of terror. He was not in danger of going to prison or losing his fortune, but he was in great danger of being called a hypocrite in front of the people of Middlemarch – and, worse, his wife.

Mr Bulstrode had started as a young banker's clerk, clever with numbers and words, preaching at a small church in his spare time. That was the happiest time of his life. At the church, he met Mr Dunkirk, a very rich man with a city business, who lived in a fine house in London. Young Nicholas Bulstrode became a favourite, especially with Mrs Dunkirk, and was soon offered a good job in the Dunkirks' business, which he accepted.

The business was a pawnbroker's, with offices in London's best streets. Mr Bulstrode soon became aware that money was often lent against goods that were known to be stolen. So the young man found himself living two separate lives: from Monday to Saturday he was making money from the poor and mixing with criminals; on Sunday he was preaching God's word. He persuaded himself that God wished him to follow this path, so that he could use the fortune he was building to help others.

Years before, the Dunkirks' only daughter had run away from home and gone on the stage. Their only son now died, and then Mr Dunkirk died too. Young Bulstrode was at the centre of the business and became the manager, and soon there was talk of marriage to the widow, Mrs Dunkirk. It was known that the daughter, Sarah, had married a Pole. The widow wanted to find her, and Mr Bulstrode advertised widely. He told Mrs Dunkirk that Sarah could not be found, and was probably dead, and so she married Mr Bulstrode, leaving her money to him in her will.

In fact, the daughter *had* been found. Only one man knew that besides Mr Bulstrode, and that man was John Raffles, who was paid to keep silent and go to America. Mr Bulstrode persuaded himself that the money would be wasted on an actress who had married a foreigner; he, Mr Bulstrode, would use it in God's service. After Mrs Dunkirk, now Mrs Bulstrode, died, Mr Bulstrode continued the pawnbroking business, gradually taking out his money until the business went bankrupt, and then he moved to Middlemarch, where he became the respectable Bulstrode, banker and churchman. But now his past rose up in front of him like a great snake, in the shape of John Raffles.

Mr Bulstrode thought of a way to make things right, and he invited Will Ladislaw to his office. Will was shocked by Mr Bulstrode's changed appearance.

'Under the law, Mr Ladislaw, you have no claim against me. Sarah Dunkirk, your mother, disappeared, and your father died from illness,' the banker explained. 'But Sarah's mother became my first wife. I became rich from that marriage, because your mother couldn't be found.'

Will felt disgusted and angry, and stood up, ready to leave.

'Please sit down, Mr Ladislaw,' said the banker. 'I am sure you are surprised by this discovery. I know that you have no fortune, and I wish now to give you a part of your grandmother's money.'

'I imagine that you looked for my mother?' said Will.

Mr Bulstrode did not answer because he dared not tell a lie. 'I will allow you five hundred pounds a year, Mr Ladislaw, and a sum of money on my death.'

'I believe you were employed in my grandparents' pawnbroker's and you did business with thieves,' said Will, bitterly. 'My honour is important to me. Thank you for giving me the opportunity to refuse this money, and to remain a gentleman. Goodbye, sir.'

Mr Bulstrode shook violently. His only comfort was that Will Ladislaw was unlikely to make public what he now knew.

There was talk in Middlemarch about Will, but not in relation to Mr Bulstrode or Raffles. The talk reached Dorothea when she visited Freshitt Hall, and met her neighbour Mrs Cadwallader as she was leaving.

'Young Ladislaw hasn't left Middlemarch, and isn't going, it seems,' said Mrs Cadwallader. 'Whenever anyone visits the Lydgate house, there he is, singing at the piano with Mrs Lydgate.'

'I don't believe it,' said Dorothea. 'I won't hear any evil spoken of Mr Ladislaw; he has already suffered enough injustice!'

On her way home, tears rolled down Dorothea's face. 'It isn't true!' she cried inside, but she could not forget the memory of seeing Will and Mrs Lydgate together.

When she reached home and found Will waiting to see her, it was like finding a much-loved object that had been lost. But she could not forget Mrs Cadwallader's words.

'I thought we said goodbye some weeks ago,' said Dorothea.

'Things have changed,' said Will, his voice shaking. 'Then I was dreaming that I might come back one day. Now I don't think I ever will. I have been insulted in your eyes and the eyes of your friends. I would never give others the chance to say that I was using you to get your money.' He went to the window.

'I have always trusted you,' said Dorothea.

Words lay unspoken between them.

'I must go,' said Will, full of bitter feeling. 'I can't have what I care for most in life, so I shall accept the first job that is offered to me. I suppose one can work without happiness or hope.'

He paused, imagining that Dorothea must understand that he meant her. But Dorothea did not understand – she thought he meant Rosamond Lydgate.

They spoke a few more words but did not hear each other.

'I am leaving Middlemarch the day after tomorrow,' said

Will, his hand on the door.

'Please remember me,' said Dorothea, holding back her tears.

'You are the only one I will remember,' said Will.

And he left her. He did not think she loved him, and he could not bear the pain.

'Will ...,' she said, but he had already gone. She sank into a chair. A storm of emotions shook her body. First, there was joy. This time she could not mistake his meaning. Will loved *her*. '*You* are the only I will remember,' he had said. Then there was bitter sadness. He had gone, and her husband's mean spirit had driven him away.

Chapter 7   A Great Fall

Christmas that year for Lydgate was not a happy one. Nothing less than a thousand pounds would free him from his troubles. As the new year came, and Middlemarch tradesmen expected to be paid for services and goods provided in the old year, Lydgate was hardly able to think of anything else. His bitter moods separated him more and more from Rosamond, who had made no attempt to manage the house more carefully. He suggested that they should offer their house to Ned Plymdale, who was now engaged, and find a smaller one.

'Sir Godwin was very kind to me when we visited after our wedding,' said Rosamond. 'Tell him about our problems; he will do something. We can't give up our house to Ned Plymdale! He once asked me to marry him and I refused.'

'I would prefer to give up my house than make a fool of myself by begging from Sir Godwin,' said Lydgate angrily.

So Rosamond wrote to Sir Godwin, asking for money, without telling her husband, and sat back calmly to wait for his reply. Sir Godwin had thought her very pretty on their visit, and had said so to her, and she was sure he would be pleased to help his nephew.

After three more weeks of bills arriving and no hope of paying them, Lydgate decided that he would have to ask his uncle. He was going to tell Rosamond of his decision, when she ran to him with a letter. It was addressed to him, from Sir Godwin.

'Dear Tertius,' it read. 'Don't tell your wife to write to me. It is not the action of a gentleman. I never choose to write to a woman on matters of business. I cannot provide the thousand pounds she has requested, or even half that sum. With three sons and three daughters, my own family takes every penny.'

Lydgate shook with anger. 'We cannot live together if you are always acting in secret behind my back,' he said to his wife.

It was a terrible moment in Rosamond's young life. Her husband, Sir Godwin, the tradesmen and her father – they were all unkind. There was only one blameless person in Rosamond's world, and that was Rosamond herself.

'I only wanted to help,' she cried. 'It is hard to feel ashamed among our friends, and to live in such a poor way. Why didn't I die with the baby!'

Lydgate took her in his arms. It was ten times harder for her than for him – he understood that now. She was a weak woman. He did not understand that all the power was in Rosamond's hands. He never thought of his medical studies now, only of how to get money. And so he found himself in a Middlemarch pub, playing a game of billiards. His disapproval of Mr Farebrother's betting at cards was forgotten, as he began to win money by betting himself. He became feverish as he played game after game, and soon passed the point where his luck turned and he began to lose. Desperate to win again, he missed shot after shot, and all the men in the pub gathered to watch. By chance, Rosamond's brother Fred came into the pub at that moment. In the past, Fred had spent too much time in the pub, and he recognised the wild look in Lydgate's eye.

'Lydgate,' he said, stepping forward. 'There's a man out here who needs some medical attention. Come and help him.'

The next morning, Lydgate was disgusted with himself. The only possibility now was to forget his pride and ask Mr Bulstrode for a loan. His debts were so serious that even the butcher and the baker would soon refuse to supply him.

Not long after that, Mr Bulstrode called him to the bank to ask his advice about a new plan to move to the seaside for his health. Lydgate had to agree that Mr Bulstrode's health was poor, made worse recently by an inability to sleep. At the same time, Mr Bulstrode informed him that Mrs Casaubon was going to take over his role as chief financial supporter of the new hospital. Lydgate was privately pleased with both of these developments, since he disliked Mr Bulstrode, but he felt he must take this opportunity to ask the banker to lend him a thousand pounds.

The banker listened to the doctor's problems in silence. 'My advice to you, Mr Lydgate,' he said, 'is not to get into further debt, but to become bankrupt. In time, you can start again in a different business – perhaps open a chemist's.'

Lydgate thanked him bitterly for his advice and left.

The direct cause of Mr Bulstrode's worsening health was not lack of sleep, but John Raffles, who was now visiting Middlemarch weekly and usually drunk, threatening to tell Mrs Bulstrode everything. Mr Bulstrode had one hope. He noticed that Raffles's health was much worse since that first payment of two hundred pounds; he might be drinking himself to death.

Just after Lydgate had left Mr Bulstrode's office without the thousand pounds, a message arrived at the bank saying that Mr Raffles was at Stone Court again, and that he seemed seriously ill. Mr Bulstrode sent for Lydgate to meet him at Stone Court, jumped up on his horse and rode there at once.

'I have called you to examine an unfortunate man who I employed many years ago,' he told Lydgate when the doctor arrived. 'He has become a drunk and is now seriously ill; his mind is affected. I feel I must do what I can for him.'

Lydgate examined the patient and reported to Mr Bulstrode that the patient was seriously ill, but would not die. He must be carefully watched, however, and kept away from alcohol; one more bottle might kill him.

'I will stay and look after him myself,' said Bulstrode. 'My housekeeper, Mrs Abel, can help me if necessary.'

Lydgate was surprised, but gave his medical directions to the banker. 'He will pass through a worse stage, when he cries out for alcohol, but he will probably get better in a few days. It is usual practice to give more alcohol to help recovery from alcohol poisoning, but I believe that is wrong, and recent medical studies support me.'

As he rode home, Lydgate thought how kind Mr Bulstrode was to this desperate drunk, after he had been so unkind to Lydgate that morning. He prepared to tell Rosamond that his last hope was gone. But when he arrived, Dover's men were in the house, ready to take away the furniture. Rosamond was lying on her bed, empty of tears and empty of love for her husband.

'Forgive me for this unhappiness!' said Lydgate, lying on the bed beside her.

At Stone Court, Raffles struggled through the night and Mr Bulstrode sat beside him, offering him food and refusing him alcohol, as Lydgate had directed. He was aware that Raffles's death would save his reputation. He must not help the man to die, of course, but who would miss Raffles? He now regretted his refusal to lend money to Lydgate. Raffles might say something about his past while Lydgate was in the room. He needed the doctor to be his friend.

When Lydgate came at midday, the patient was crying out streams of nonsense. Lydgate gave Mr Bulstrode some medicine to give Raffles in very small amounts at times which he carefully wrote down. Too much and too often would be harmful. But Lydgate was hopeful. 'The man is strong,' he said. 'He will live.'

'You look ill yourself,' said Mr Bulstrode. 'I have been thinking about our conversation yesterday morning. Mrs Bulstrode is worried about her niece, Rosamond. I can't help everybody who asks me for a loan, Mr Lydgate, but I have decided to help you.'

And he wrote out a cheque for a thousand pounds.

A great wave of joy swept through Lydgate, pushing away every other feeling. 'I am deeply grateful to you. You have given me back my happiness and some hope of doing good in the world,' he said as he left.

After thirty-six hours without sleep, Mr Bulstrode gave the care of Raffles to his housekeeper, Mrs Abel, for the night. He repeated Lydgate's directions exactly – or almost exactly, forgetting to say how often she must give Raffles the medicine. And then he went to bed and cursed the fact that Raffles was beginning to show signs of getting better. It was about one o'clock in the morning when Mrs Abel knocked at his door.

'May I give him a drop of alcohol, sir?' asked Mrs Abel. 'He's had all the doctor's medicine. He says he can't swallow anything except a glass of wine, and he's suffering so much.'

A struggle began inside Mr Bulstrode.

'When I nursed my poor master – Mr Robinson – I had to give him a big glass of wine every hour,' said Mrs Abel. 'It helped him at the end. I think Mr Lydgate's advice is unkind.'

'It is not evil to help a man who is suffering,' thought the banker, holding out the key to the drinks cupboard.

When he woke again a few hours later, Mr Bulstrode called Mrs Abel. 'How is Mr Raffles? Is he better?' he asked.

'I'm sorry, sir,' said Mrs Abel. 'Your friend is dead.'

When tears poured from Mr Bulstrode's eyes, Mrs Abel felt sorry for him, not realising that he was crying with joy. The deeply religious banker spent some time in prayer before going into the room where Raffles lay dead. He removed the empty wine bottle and the empty medicine bottle from the bedroom and hid them. When Lydgate arrived, the doctor was surprised that he had not judged the situation correctly.

Later that day, on his way home from Stone Court, Mr Bulstrode rode past a group of tradesmen who had gathered in Middlemarch High Street to listen to a well-known horse dealer, who was in possession of a fine story.

'That's him!' whispered the horse dealer, pointing at the banker. 'I heard all about him a few weeks ago, from a man called John Raffles.'

After the horse dealer had told every detail of Raffles's story, the butcher added the news that the man had died that day at Stone Court, and that Lydgate was the doctor. The shoemaker then mentioned that Mr and Mrs Lydgate had just paid their debts and sent away Dover and his men, who had arrived the day before to start taking their furniture.

The only topic of conversation in Middlemarch for the next few days was the fall of the 'hypocrite Mr Bulstrode'. The Middlemarch doctors could not criticise Lydgate or Mrs Abel for following the usual practice of giving medicine and alcohol. The timing of the loan to Lydgate, however, was more than enough to give the whole story 'an ugly look'.

Mr Bulstrode was finished in Middlemarch. Was Lydgate finished with him? The younger man regretted coming to this town. He would have returned the thousand pounds if he had not already paid his debts with it. He decided, however, that he would not run away from the angry looks and whispered words. He would show that he was a man, and that he was not afraid.

Not everyone believed the worst of Lydgate. When Dorothea heard the story of Mr Bulstrode and Lydgate from her uncle, she said, 'Let us find out the truth.'

Chapter 8   Sunset and Sunrise

Although Rosamond was pleased to be rescued from Dover and his men, she felt no joy. Her husband's moods grew darker and her life was spoiled. She wanted to move away, to London. At the same time, she missed Will. She had decided that he was secretly in love with her, and only pretended to admire Mrs Casaubon to make her jealous.

A letter came from Will, suggesting a short visit to Middlemarch to discuss some business with Lydgate. He hoped to make music with Rosamond and enjoy his place on the carpet by the fire.

Will's letter lifted her mood, and Rosamond decided to have a dinner party. She sent out invitations to some of the more important people in Middlemarch, and the next morning several replies came by post. She sat down cheerfully to open them and then make a seating plan for the dinner. Her smile soon left her face, however, as each letter was a refusal. And then she realised that in the last few days she had had no visitors, not even her mother. People had stared at her oddly in the town.

The poor girl went straight to see her parents to ask if they could explain it. Her mother cried as her father told her the whole story.

'So you know everything about Bulstrode and Raffles,' said Lydgate, when she returned home.

He waited for her to say that she loved him, that she was sure he was not guilty of taking money in exchange for his silence. But Rosamond did not think of his problems – only of her own.

'I can't continue living in Middlemarch, Tertius,' she replied. 'We *must* go to London.'

Since Mr Bulstrode was continuing with his plans to leave the new hospital, Dorothea asked Lydgate to come and see her to discuss the future. She did not really want to discuss the hospital; she wanted to express her belief in him.

She had not seen Lydgate for two months and was shocked at the change in him. She asked him to explain what had really happened. Dorothea's was the first friendly voice that Lydgate had heard since the death of Raffles. He told her the whole story. Lydgate had been pronounced guilty by the people of Middlemarch because they did not like him, because he had worked for Mr Bulstrode and because he had taken the banker's money.

'I believe in you, Mr Lydgate. I would like to continue the present plan for the hospital,' said Dorothea. 'I will provide the money – I have much more than I need and I must use it for a good purpose. The bad feeling towards you will gradually disappear when people see the good you are doing.'

'I am very grateful, Mrs Casaubon,' said Lydgate sadly, 'but I have to consider my wife's happiness. She wishes to leave Middlemarch. The fact is, we have not been able to speak properly about the trouble, and I don't know what she believes about me.'

'May I go and see her?' said Dorothea eagerly. 'I will tell her that you are blameless. If she learns that you have friends who support you, she may feel happy to stay.'

'Thank you, but I must do as other men do. I must think
what will please the world and bring us some money. I will
look for work in London, where there are plenty of rich, lazy
people who need doctors. I will find a shell and hide in it.'

'It is not brave,' said Dorothea, 'to give up the fight.'

'I have no choice,' said Lydgate. 'But you have given me
courage. If you can persuade some of my friends, especially Mr
Farebrother, that I have not taken money in exchange for my
silence, and if you could visit my wife, I will be very grateful.'

As Lydgate rode away, Dorothea thought of another way she
could help him. She sat down and wrote out a cheque for a
thousand pounds, to deliver to Rosamond the next day.

The following morning, she had a long conversation with
Mr Farebrother, who joyfully accepted her explanation of
his friend Lydgate's behaviour. Then Dorothea went into
Middlemarch to visit Mrs Lydgate. The Lydgates had only one
servant now, and she was standing at the open front door.

'Is Mrs Lydgate at home?' asked Dorothea.

'I'm not sure, my lady,' said the girl. 'She went to the post
earlier. She might be upstairs. Please come in and I'll look.'

The girl pushed open the door to the sitting room,
without going in, and waited for Dorothea to enter, before
running upstairs.

Dorothea walked into the room. She looked at the scene
before her and lost her power of speech.

Seated with his back to her on the sofa was Will Ladislaw.
Next to him, in tears, and with her hands in his, was
Rosamond.

Dorothea made a slight noise as she tried to back out of the
room. Rosamond pulled her hands back and jumped up. As Will
turned and his eyes met Dorothea's, he seemed to turn to stone.

'Excuse me, Mrs Lydgate, the servant thought you were

out,' Dorothea managed to say. 'I have brought a letter for Mr Lydgate.'

She put it on a small table and was gone.

Will and Rosamond stood in silence. Rosamond could see that Will had received a shock, but she had never imagined another human being's state of mind except in relation to her. She believed he only needed a kind word from her. She put her hand on his arm.

'Don't touch me!' Will shouted in extreme anger. 'I had no hope before, but I had one certainty – that she trusted me. Whatever people said, she believed the best of me. That's gone! No other woman exists by the side of her. I would prefer to kiss her hand if she were dead than kiss the hand of any living woman.'

Rosamond had never experienced such terror. Will's poisonous words struck her heart and she understood that she had been wrong – that he had never loved her.

That night, Dorothea lay on the cold stone floor of her bedroom and cried bitter tears. In the depth of her sadness she discovered how much she had loved Will, and how angry she was that he had cared so little for her. She cried all night. But she had never felt pity for herself, and her reason returned with the morning light. By eleven o'clock she had recovered and was on the road to Middlemarch, hoping again to see and help Rosamond.

Lydgate himself was in the hall when Dorothea was announced. It was clear that he knew nothing of the previous day's visit, and he thanked Dorothea sincerely for her kindness in lending him the money. Dorothea was delighted to hear that the cheque was going to Mr Bulstrode that morning, to repay that loan. When Rosamond came downstairs, Lydgate left the women together.

Dorothea had imagined herself to be stronger than she was,

and had to control her tears. But after a few moments, she was able to talk about the injustice that Lydgate had suffered from Middlemarch. She told Rosamond that he had friends who admired him – herself, Mr Farebrother, Mr Brooke, Sir James. She spoke of Lydgate's love for his wife, and his sorrow that he had brought her so much trouble. Rosamond felt that she was in the presence of a superior being. Dorothea's gentle kindness affected her more than the cruellest words, and she burst into violent cries.

'Tertius is so angry if I say anything,' said Rosamond when she was calm again. 'How can I talk to him about painful subjects?'

'I hoped that your husband would stay at the new hospital,' Dorothea continued. 'But he has refused, because life in Middlemarch has become too painful for you. He says you will move to London. I know that marriage can be hard, but it is worth fighting for. You may think that you are in love with Mr Ladislaw, and that life with him would be better, but do you really want to destroy your marriage and your good name? I know it is hard – we are weak, I am weak –'

Dorothea was deathly pale and could say nothing more. Rosamond leaned forward and kissed her forehead, and they held each other like two drowning women.

'You are thinking something that isn't true,' whispered Rosamond, with unusual unselfishness. 'When you came into the room yesterday, Mr Ladislaw was telling me that he loved another woman, and could never love me. And now he hates me because you must think he is a bad person. He said yesterday that no woman exists for him except you. I am sorry. The misunderstanding is all my fault.'

At that moment, Lydgate appeared at the door.

'I thought you looked pale this morning, Mrs Casaubon,' he said. 'I noticed that you walked here, and I think it might rain.

Can I send someone for your carriage to collect you?'

'Oh no! I am strong. I need the walk,' said Dorothea. 'Mrs Lydgate and I have chatted, and now I must go.'

'Well, Rosy,' he said, after Dorothea had gone, 'what do you think of Mrs Casaubon?'

'I think she is wonderful,' said Rosamond. 'But she is so beautiful, she will make you more unhappy with me than ever!'

'But has she made *you* less unhappy with *me*?' he asked.

'I think she has,' said Rosamond, kissing his cheek.

Will had returned to Middlemarch to see Dorothea, but after his terrible visit to Rosamond, he decided to return to London. When his anger had calmed, however, he felt that it would be cruel to go without speaking to Rosamond again. He went to the Lydgates' home for dinner, but he had no chance to speak to Rosamond alone. Then, when he was leaving, she put a note into his hand.

Will's fear turned to joy and then to doubt as he read her words: 'I have told Mrs Casaubon that there is nothing between us. She came to see me again and was very kind. You have nothing to blame me for now.'

The following morning, while Dorothea sat in the library trying to read a book on political economy, her servant announced Will's arrival. Dorothea jumped up in alarm and excitement.

'Thank you for seeing me,' Will said, when he came into the library.

'I wanted to see you,' she said.

They sat and looked at each other, both their hearts filled with their hopeless love.

'I don't doubt you,' said Dorothea, reaching out her hand.

Will took her hand and kissed it. 'Now we can at least

speak to each other honestly,' he said. 'Even if you loved me as much as I love you, I will always be poor. We must always be divided. I intended to go away into silence, but as you see I have failed.'

'Don't be sorry,' said Dorothea. 'I would prefer us to share our troubles.'

Will pulled her towards him, and they kissed. They sat holding hands, both full of thoughts that they could not speak.

'It is impossible!' cried Will angrily, jumping up and moving towards the door. 'We can never be married.'

'I can't bear it,' said Dorothea. 'My heart will break. I don't mind being poor – I don't want Mr Casaubon's money. We could live well on my own money. I need so little ... I will learn what everything costs.'

'But Dorothea, you are a lady. You can't give everything up and live in a small house, perhaps an ugly house in a city, away from this beautiful countryside.'

'How can I live here alone? The countryside has no beauty if *you* are not in it.'

'Your family hates me. Sir James refuses to speak to me. He may not speak to you if you marry me. You won't be able to see Celia.'

'Then we will go away and not see them,' said Dorothea. 'I can't live without you.'

♦

The years passed. Lydgate eventually gained an excellent medical practice in London with a good income from rich patients. People admired his charming wife and fine house and said he was a successful man, but he thought of himself as a failure. He died when he was only fifty, leaving his wife and children with plenty of money. Soon after that, Rosamond married an older man and often spoke of her happiness as a 'reward'.

Dorothea was never sorry that she had given up her position in society and her fortune to marry Will, although Sir James at first refused to accept him into the family. Their love for each other was stronger than anything that could spoil it. Will worked hard for political reform, and eventually became a Member of Parliament. Dorothea loved the life, helping her husband to correct some of the many wrongs that existed in society.

When Dorothea wrote to Celia to tell her that she had given birth to a little boy, Celia burst into violent tears.

'I can't see my sister's baby and tell her how to bring him up properly,' cried Celia. 'She will do everything wrong!'

Sir James was so affected by his wife's unhappiness that he immediately invited Dorothea and her husband to visit. Sir James never liked Will, but it was soon understood that Mr and Mrs Ladislaw would stay at Tipton Grange twice a year. Visits from there to Freshitt Hall allowed Dorothea and Celia to spend time together and the young cousins to play. When Mr Brooke died after a long life, Tipton was inherited by Dorothea's son, who managed the estate well and enjoyed the life of a country gentleman.

The people of Middlemarch spoke of Dorothea Brooke as a fine girl who married a sick clergyman who was old enough to be her father, and then gave up her estate to marry his poor young cousin. They could not understand why she had ever married either of them.

ACTIVITIES

Chapter 1

Before you read

1 Discuss these questions.

    a There are two unhappy marriages in this story. How many reasons can you think of why a marriage can go wrong?

    b This story takes place in England in about 1830, when women did not have the same rights as men. In your country, are there ways in which women today are not equal to men? How was the situation different two hundred years ago?

2 Look at the Word List at the back of the book. Discuss the meanings of unfamiliar words, and then answer these questions.

    a Have you ever inherited anything? What was it? What would you *like* to inherit?

    b Can you name a hypocrite from a film or a book – or from real life? In what ways is he or she hypocritical?

    c How should people treat their tenants, and the buildings that their tenants live or work in?

While you read

3 Which of these facts about Dorothea are true (T)?

    a She lives with her uncle because her parents are living abroad.   .....

    b She is 21.   .....

    c She has her own money.   .....

    d She often behaves in a way that is surprising for a young lady.   .....

    e She expects to marry a country gentleman like Sir James.   .....

    f She cannot ride a horse.   .....

4 Who is speaking?

    a 'Think of the poor men who have to dig those stones out of the ground.'   ....

b 'Young ladies don't understand
economics. Nor history.'   ....

c 'I spend my time reading ancient
languages.'   ....

d 'Dorothea likes giving things up.'   ....

e 'I am sure that Miss Brooke's reasons
are admirable.'   ....

f 'I would learn to see the truth and to
think like great men.'   ....

g 'Everyone except you can see that he
is in love with you.'   ....

h 'He is not young, my dear, and his
health is poor.'   ....

After you read

5 Discuss your answers to Activity 4, above. Who or what
are these people talking about?

6 How are these people different from each other?

   a Dorothea and Celia.

   b Sir James and Mr Casaubon.

7 Work in pairs. Have this conversation.

   Student A: You are Sir James. Tell Mr Brooke that you
would like to marry Dorothea.

   Student B: You are Mr Brooke. Tell Sir James that Dorothea
has accepted Mr Casaubon's offer of marriage.
Try to explain why.

Chapter 2

Before you read

8 Discuss these questions. What do you think?

   a An ambitious young doctor comes to Middlemarch.
How will the townspeople, and the other doctors, react
to his new medical ideas?

   b Why might Dorothea change her mind about marrying
Mr Casaubon?

9 Complete the sentences with the correct names.

a .... comes from a good family, but is poor.

b .... is dying.

c .... hopes to inherit Stone Court.

d .... is ashamed of her family.

e .... wants to add to scientific knowledge.

f .... lives according to very strict moral principles.

g .... does not wish to marry for several years.

h .... loses the vote for hospital clergyman.

10 Are these statements correct (✓) or wrong (✗)?

a Dorothea is delighted with married life.   .....

b Mr Casaubon is delighted with married life.   .....

c Mr Casaubon is making no progress with writing his great book   .....

d Dorothea is pleased to spend time with Will Ladislaw in Rome.   .....

e Will enjoys Dorothea's company.   .....

f Mr Casaubon is very pleased that Dorothea enjoys his cousin's company.   .....

g Celia is going to marry Sir James.   .....

h Will is planning a new life back in England.   .....

After you read

11 Who do you think should really be married to whom? Consider the different possibilities, and choose the best marriage partners.

Lydgate	Will Ladislaw	Sir James	Mr Casaubon
Dorothea	Celia	Rosamond	

Chapter 3

Before you read

12 Discuss these questions.

a How does Will's opinion of Mr Casaubon's work affect

87

Dorothea's opinion of it?

b How does Dorothea's idea of duty differ from her husband's?

c What will her life be like when she and Mr Casaubon return from their honeymoon?

While you read

13 Find the best ending below (1–6) to each sentence.

a Lydgate offends another doctor by   .....

b Rosamond is impressed by   .....

c Mr Casaubon angers Dorothea by   .....

d Mr Casaubon is in danger of   .....

e Mr Brooke confuses the situation with Will by   .....

1) … sudden death.

2) … treating Fred Vincy.

3) … showing unreasonable jealousy.

4) … Lydgate's manners and good taste.

5) … inviting him to visit.

14 Write these words in the sentences below.

angry   beautiful   depressed   more interesting

more suitable   sorry

a Lydgate thinks that Dorothea is ....

b He finds the cases of poor patients .... than those of his rich patients.

c Mrs Bulstrode thinks that Ned Plymdale would make a .... husband for her niece than Lydgate.

d Lydgate is .... when he hears the talk about himself and Rosamond.

e Rosamond is .... when Lydgate stops visiting her.

f Lydgate becomes engaged to Rosamond because he feels .... for her.

15 Circle the mistake in each sentence and then correct it.

a Mr Brooke has invited Will to Tipton Grange for a few days.

....

b Mr Featherstone leaves Stone Court to his cousin.

....

88

c Mr Vincy plans to pay for his daughter's new home.

....

d Lydgate expects to receive several hundred pounds from Sir Godwin. ....

After you read

16 Lydgate is getting into debt – and personal debt is, of course, a common problem. Work in small groups. Imagine that each of you owes money, for different reasons. Explain your situation to the other members of the group and ask for advice.

Chapter 4

Before you read

17 This chapter is called 'Politics, Prison and Poison'. Discuss these questions.

a Which characters will get involved in politics? Why? How successful will they be?

b Which characters will seem like prisoners in their homes, or in Middlemarch?

c Whose mind will continue to be poisoned by negative thoughts? What effect will that have on others?

While you read

18 Choose the best words in *italics*, and circle them.

a Will has a new career in *the law / political journalism*.

b Will's grandfather was *an Italian actor / a Polish teacher*.

c Will's *mother / father* also ran away from home, but for more mysterious reasons.

d Mr Casaubon is *pleased / displeased* when he hears about Will's new job.

e After Mr Dagley's insults, Mr Brooke finally hires *a secretary / an estate manager* at Tipton Grange.

f *Will / Mr Casaubon* tells Dorothea that Will has been forbidden to visit Lowick Manor.

g Joshua Rigg gives his stepfather *what he wants / very little*.

h Mr Casaubon learns that he *will / may* die soon.

19 Answer the questions.

    a Who would like to be a Member of Parliament?

    b Which paper supports social reform: the *Pioneer* or the *Trumpet*?

    c Who feels that he/she is in prison, but denies it?

    d Who feels that poison is spreading inside him/her?

Chapter 5

Before you read

20 Discuss these questions. What do you think?

    a John Raffles has picked up a piece of paper from the fireplace at Stone Court. How might this be important?

    b Mr Casaubon has 'other weapons to try' against Will. What is he planning?

While you read

21 Who do the words in *italics* refer to?

    a Dorothea to herself: 'Why were *they* alone together?'

    ....

    b Will to Rosamond: 'When one sees *a perfect woman*, one never thinks of her character.'

    ....

    c Rosamond: '*You* like your work better than me.'

    ....

    d Lydgate to Farebrother: '*They* will not drive me away.'

    ....

    e Dorothea to herself: 'I cannot break *his* heart. I must say yes.'

    ....

22 Write *Bulstrode* or *Raffles* in the spaces.

    a Joshua Rigg sells Stone Court to ...., who doesn't move there.

    b .... feels that he has paid for his past mistakes.

    c .... nearly faints when he sees

.... outside Stone Court.

d ....'s first name is Nick, short for Nicholas.

e .... saw ....'s name on a piece of paper at Stone Court.

f .... has been paid for years to keep ....'s secrets, and to stay away.

g .... wouldn't be rich now without ....'s help in the past.

h .... goes away with two hundred pounds.

After you read

23 Complete these sentences with one or more suitable adjectives, and then compare your answers with another student's.

a When Mr Casaubon dies, Dorothea feels ...

b When she reads his will, she feels ...

c Mr Casaubon's plan to keep Will away will be ...

d Will wants to be with Dorothea, but feels ...

Chapter 6

Before you read

24 How do you think that Mr Bulstrode and Will are connected? What effect might their connection have on the future of these two characters?

While you read

25 Are these sentences true (T) or false (F)?

a Dorothea plans to continue her husband's work. .....

b Will and Dorothea do not tell each other their real feelings. .....

c Lydgate is delighted to welcome Captain Lydgate to his home. .....

d Rosamond ignores her husband's wishes about riding. .....

e Will learns the truth about his cousin's will from Rosamond. .....

    f He learns the truth about his mother's family
       from Mr Bulstrode. .....

    g He refuses Mr Bulstrode's offer of money. .....

    h Dorothea finally understands that Will is in love
       with her. .....

After you read

  26 Draw a family tree for Will Ladislaw. Include information that
     you have about his parents and grandparents.

  27 Discuss these questions with a partner.

    a Who is more to blame for their debt: Rosamond or Lydgate?

    b Why does John Raffles try to make friends with Will?

    c Why is Mr Bulstrode in danger of being called a hypocrite?

Chapters 7–8

Before you read

  28 Discuss how you think the story will end for each of the main
     characters.

While you read

  29 Put these events in the order they happen (1–8).

    a Lydgate tries betting. .....

    b John Raffles dies; Lydgate is his doctor. .....

    c Sir Godwin writes to Lydgate. .....

    d Dorothea learns from Rosamond that Will loves
       her. .....

    e Dorothea visits Rosamond and finds Will there. .....

    f Rosamond writes to Sir Godwin. .....

    g Mr Bulstrode lends Lydgate money. .....

    h Mr Bulstrode refuses Lydgate a loan. .....

After you read

  30 Read the last five lines of the story again. Then discuss
     whether you have a greater understanding of Dorothea's
     reasons than the people of Middlemarch.

Writing

  31 Imagine that Lydgate and Dorothea meet before she is engaged
     to Mr Casaubon, and that they get married. Write a paragraph

describing their married life.

32 Dorothea and Mr Casaubon go to Rome for their honeymoon. The Lydgates visit the country estate of Sir Godwin Lydgate. In what ways are these choices satisfactory or unsatisfactory for the newly-married couples?

33 Will Ladislaw edits and writes for a reforming newspaper, the *Pioneer*. Write, for a similar newspaper, about something that needs to be changed in your society today.

34 If Lydgate had controlled his spending, and Rosamond's, from the day of their engagement, their lives in Middlemarch would have been very different. Explain how.

35 In Chapter 6, Sir James interrupts a conversation between Will and Dorothea. Re-read this conversation. Then imagine that Sir James's visit is delayed for half an hour by a shower of rain. Continue their conversation.

36 In Chapter 7, Rosamond writes to Sir Godwin Lydgate, asking for money. Write her letter.

37 Dorothea and Celia are unable to meet for several years after Dorothea marries Will. Write a conversation between the two sisters when they finally meet again.

38 Imagine that you are going to make a film of Middlemarch – in English or in your own language. Choose actors for the main parts, and explain your choices.

39 Imagine that you are a time traveller, and your time machine takes you back to Middlemarch in 1830. Write a comparison between life in England then and now.

40 George Eliot's characters are complicated human beings; her heroes have faults as well as strengths. Choose one of these characters and list their admirable and less admirable qualities: Dorothea; Will; Lydgate.

WORD LIST

approve (v) to believe that something is good or acceptable

aware (adj) knowing about or realising something

bankrupt (adj) unable to pay your debts, so unable to continue in business

baronet (n) a member of the upper class in Britain with the title 'Sir'; after a baronet's death, the title passes to his eldest son

billiards (n) a game played on a large table covered in cloth, usually a green one. Players hit balls into pockets around the table with a long stick.

carriage (n) a vehicle with wheels pulled by horses

clergyman (n) a person who works for the church

cottage (n) a small house, especially in the country

engagement (n) an agreement to get married. After they have made this agreement, a couple are **engaged**.

estate (n) a large area of land in the countryside with one large house on it

frog (n) a small green animal that lives near water and has long legs for jumping

honeymoon (n) a holiday after a wedding

hypocrite (n) a person who pretends to be something that they are not

idealist (n) a person who believes that you should live according to high principles, even when it is difficult

impressed (adj) admiring something or someone

inherit (v) to receive money, a house or other possessions after someone has died. If you are **disinherited** by your family, you receive nothing.

loan (n) an amount of money that you borrow

manufacture (v) to make things using machines, and sell them

myth (n) an ancient story that explains how humans or the world became what they are

pawnbroker's (n) a business that lends money to people in exchange for their possessions

preach (v) to make a speech about a religious subject, usually in a church